PORK

ORK

CRIS
FREDDI

Routledge & Kegan Paul
London and Henley

First published in Great Britain in 1982
by Routledge & Kegan Paul Ltd
39 Store Street, London WC1E 7DD and
Broadway House, Newtown Road,
Henley-on-Thames, Oxon RG9 1EN
Printed in Great Britain by
Redwood Burn Ltd, Trowbridge, Wiltshire
Copyright © 1981 by Cris Freddi

ISBN 0–7100–9230–X

For Les Milkins

CONTENTS

Somewhere in the damp deciduous north there was a forest like any other, a place where the animals could walk and talk and sometimes die, and wake up too soon during hibernation. . . .

PORK

PORK

IT WAS STILL VERY COLD AND THERE was rain in the air when round Pork pushed his snout out from under the leaves.

It was well into autumn and the leaves were wet, fresh-smelling. Pork frowned. Too soon, he said to himself. Waking up too soon with everything still all wet and cold. Very strange. He took a couple of steps forward, scratched at the damp forest floor, and sniffed. Too soon. Too wet. He sniffed again, coughed, and shambled off into the night.

The undergrowth was dripping wet and packed tight like the stuffing of an old mattress. It made travelling very laborious for someone as short as Pork, but he was a robust and dogged animal and the undergrowth was his home. He squared his shoulders, bustled on, and reached a small clearing surrounded by beech trees.

And here he stopped for a breather, looking around

with his nose twitching at the air. A small fat raindrop flipped down from the trees and hit his forehead. He opened his mouth for a moment, nosed briefly at the rotting foliage under his feet, and set off again.

"You!"

He'd only just started to move when the cry sprang out across the clearing. It was a shrill cry, and when Pork turned his head slowly to the left, he saw a young squirrel squatting on a log by the roots of a tree.

Pork had seen grey squirrels before, so the sight of this one didn't frighten him. Indeed, it seemed more wary of him as he approached it, shuffling through the wet leaves. When he was quite close he stopped and looked at it. And it looked at him. And they looked at each other without so much as a twitch or a word of greeting.

It was a thin little squirrel, rather hunched and rat-like on its log. Its eyes never stopped moving.

"Who are you and what are you doing here?"

The words bundled out of its tight little mouth, one on top of the other, and Pork had trouble working out exactly what it had said. He looked at the ground.

"Well?" said the squirrel, impatiently.

"Hedgehog," said Pork, because that's what he was.

The squirrel was not impressed.

"I can see that," it said. "But what are you doing here?"

Pork looked up for a second, then stared at his feet.

"Cold," he muttered. "Woke up too soon. Wet and cold."

The squirrel twitched on its log and said nothing. Pork said nothing too, just shifted his weight from one front foot to the other while the squirrel frowned at him and waited.

"And where are you going now?" it said at last.

Pork lifted his head. Where are you going now? He licked his lips and sniffed rather loudly. Where was he going? He had no idea.

"Hedgehog," he said, but he knew it wasn't much of an answer so he looked away.

There was nothing to look at, really. Only the trees standing dripping themselves dry. And a soft cold mist beginning to rise from the wet undergrowth. It was a thin mist, barely visible, and Pork didn't see it.

He didn't see the squirrel either when he looked up. The little creature was gone, its patience exhausted, and the hedgehog wasn't surprised. For a moment or two he stood and eyed the bare log where the squirrel had been crouching. Then he walked away.

He walked for a long time, clambering up wet slippery grassbanks and pushing with difficulty through brambles and ditches piled high with leaves, pausing at intervals to catch his breath and scratch at his damp belly. When he emerged from yet another barricade of tree roots, there was a leaf stuck on his spines and it swayed in the air as he walked.

After a time, the moon came out, edging its shoulder round a cloud. Its light was too weak to break through the roof of huddled treetops, so Pork didn't know it was there. He scrummaged his way out from the edge of the forest and stopped on a flat patch of grass, exhausted.

Even when the moon swept right out from behind the clouds, Pork paid no attention to it. Tired though he was, it occurred to him that he ought to make up his mind about his next move, and he looked up to see where he was.

He had his back to the forest. Just ahead of him the grassbank dipped and came to an end. Then there was a wide ditch and, beyond that, acres of dimly lit ploughland.

But all this meant nothing to round Pork. His interest had suddenly been stirred by something in the distance, beyond all those ploughed spaces. He smiled at it.

Almost on the horizon, way out in front of him, lay a shining shape. Pork had no idea what it was, but he knew he liked it. It lay flat on the ground, twisting along between two fields. Far away and unbelievably bright. The hedgehog grinned as he stood there, his eyes fixed on the gleaming apparition. He moved forward—and then there was a sudden noise in the undergrowth behind him that stopped him in his tracks.

They came bundling out from the bracken: two of them, both young, both badgers, puffing and blowing and barking happily as they wrestled. Pork turned slowly round and stood watching them for a moment. They were badgers, and he knew badgers meant trouble for hedgehogs, but he wasn't afraid. So he turned away again and eyed the bright shape in the distance.

He eyed it so intently that he didn't see the larger of the two badgers rise to its feet and look around. He didn't see it catch sight of him as he stood there staring out across the fields. And he didn't notice it wink at its companion before trotting across the grass towards him.

"Pig!" said the badger, quite loudly and very close to Pork's ear. The hedgehog jumped, uttered a throaty little yelp and scuttled away from the direction of the voice. The badger laughed. It was a husky laugh, short and sharp and not very clever.

"Oh look," said the badger. "I frightened him. Poor hog. Poor little hedgepig."

Pork turned his head, but he kept his back to the badger as he looked at it.

"What's the matter, hedgepig?" it said as it strolled casually towards him. "Poor piglet. Not frightened, are you? Not scared, a chunky little fellow like you?"

Pork said nothing. For one thing, he was still in a mild state of shock—and besides, he was puzzled. He was slowly trying to work out why the badger had jumped on him like that, and why it was laughing as it talked to him. It was a strapping young animal, very powerful in the shoulders, and Pork watched nervously as it came right up close and towered over him with its snout almost in his face.

"Don't talk much, do you, piglet?"

Pork looked down at the ground. It was true. He didn't talk much. He licked his mouth and thought of something to say.

"Hedgehog," was all he could manage, and once again he knew it wasn't really enough.

"Oh," said the badger, in mock surprise. "A hedgehog, are you? Well, who'd have guessed it?"

Pork smiled. Perhaps, after all, the badger was impressed with his knowledge.

"Hedgehog," he said again.

The badger laughed.

"Hey!" it called, turning to its companion. "Come and say hello to our friend here."

The other badger was smaller and altogether less imposing. If anything, it looked the older of the two, but it walked with a heavy limp and had a small sour face.

"He's a hedgehog," said the bigger badger.

"I know that," said the other, gruffly. He eyed the hedgehog without enthusiasm. "What's he got that leaf stuck on his back for?"

Pork had no idea what it was talking about, but the leaf

was still there, impaled on his spines. The bigger badger smiled.

"It's only a leaf," it said. "There's nothing wrong with it. Anyway, he's probably got a good reason for wearing it. He's a clever hedgehog. Aren't you, piglet?"

By now Pork was thoroughly confused by all this talk of a leaf. He looked from one badger to the other and scratched absently at the ground.

"Cold," he said quietly. "Woke up too soon. All cold and wet."

The smaller badger spat on the grass.

"This is a right waste of time," it said with distaste. "There's no point talking to him. He's simple."

The bigger badger seemed to think this was very funny. Its shoulders shook as it laughed and beat the ground with its paw. Then quite suddenly it stopped laughing and its mood changed dramatically.

"Well of course he's simple," it said slowly. "That's what makes it so enjoyable."

It turned and stared down into the hedgehog's face. Pork looked up at it, then looked away.

"Simple," growled the badger. "That's what you are, pig. Backward."

Pork looked up again and licked his teeth. He opened his mouth to speak, but thought better of it and sniffed instead.

"Well, piglet, what do you think of that? What's it like to be a half-wit?"

No answer.

"Oh, get on with it," gruffed the smaller badger. "Finish him off. I'm starving."

The bigger badger shrugged.

"Maybe you're right," it said.

At this point, Pork felt he really ought to say something. But he didn't, because at that moment the bigger badger snarled and quite without warning struck him across the face.

It was only a glancing blow, but the badger's claws scraped across the top of Pork's nose and he squealed with the pain and the shock of it. And that seemed to goad the badger. It took another swing—and missed. It swung with the other paw, and although Pork moved to avoid it, he moved too slowly and took the full weight of it on his ear.

A hoarse piercing wind seemed to be screeching through the head of slow Pork as the force of the blow knocked him over. There were dotted lights and black shapes and a horde of confused thoughts all jostling together. Out of the corner of his eye he saw the huge badger crouching over him with its mouth open and teeth bared, but it all seemed rather unreal. He found himself obeying some vague and half-forgotten instinct and he tucked his snout into his belly, turning his back to the snarling badger as he did so.

It made little difference. The badger simply shot round to the other side of its victim, dug its paws under Pork's belly, and heaved upwards. Nothing happened. The badger grunted, dug its paws further in, and heaved again. This time it managed to lift the hedgehog up and roll him over. Pork felt himself turning upside-down and he stuffed his nose deeper into his belly, but, as it happened, the badger had heaved him so hard that he simply rolled right over and ended up lying on his stomach again, with his head pressed against the wet grass.

The badger cursed, drew back its paw, stabbed it under the hedgehog's body, and heaved with all its strength. But this time, as the hedgehog rolled over, the other badger joined in. It leapt forward and swiped at Pork's round tumbling body, grazing his side with its claws. As he tumbled, the bigger badger rushed after him, pushing his body round and round, rolling him over and over.

Pork didn't dare uncurl himself. He was too dazed and frightened to try and escape. He heard the big badger growling somewhere above him, then felt its paws digging up into his belly again. Its claws sank into his flesh and the pain jerked across his whole body. He panicked. With a twist of his hind legs he tried to move away from those savage claws, but he went the wrong way. And that, as it turned out, was the best thing he could have done.

The bigger badger had its paws under him again and was preparing to roll him once more when Pork twisted towards it and trapped one of those thick grey paws under his spiny body.

The badger's howl of pain was a loud one, and Pork was terrified. So was the badger, for it then tried to wrench its paw out from under the hedgehog's belly and only succeeded in tearing a great red gash along its thumb. It howled again, pulled its paw out, and stood there holding it up to its face, licking the wounded thumb and whimpering. The smaller badger curled its upper lip.

"Idiot," it said. "Trust you to ruin everything."

"I'm bleeding to death!" moaned the bigger badger.

"I wish you would," said the other, acidly. "Come on, let's get out of here."

And they did, making their way across the damp grass together, limping and cursing each other, and glancing back at the recumbent hedgehog before they disappeared under the hem of the forest.

Pork lay still for a long time. Very still and quiet, with his snout bleeding gently against the damp fur of his underbelly and his ear numb from the badger's attack.

When his head started to clear, he began to feel the pain of his wounds—and it dawned on him that the rain in the air was thicker. Soon it was raining hard and fast, hissing through the trees behind him and melting the ploughed fields into patches of squatting mud.

Pork raised his head and the rain hurt his nose, washing the dribbles of blood from his fur. Slowly and clumsily he hauled himself to his feet. He looked at the rain-lashed forest and thought nothing of it. He noticed that the badgers were gone, and forgot them. And when he turned away from the trees he quickly forgot the pain in his head and the cramp in his limbs.

The shining twisting shape was still there, shimmering slightly in the distance. For a moment he thought it was closer than before, but then he wasn't sure. Not that it made any difference to Pork. He stood and stared with eyes almost as bright as the shape itself. He still had no idea what it was, but he didn't care. For a while he was quite happy to just stand and look at it, ignoring the rain and his own discomforts, but then he moved forward to take a closer look.

He didn't move very far. In his excitement he'd forgotten all about the ditch that separated him from the ploughland, but now it was there again, just below him, half-hidden by straggling reeds, reminding him of its baleful presence.

Pork eyed it apprehensively—and not without reason. It really was a forbidding obstacle. There were twigs in it, it was gorged with rainwater, and it stank. It was too wide to jump over and probably too deep to wade across —and though he was quite a good swimmer the hedgehog hesitated.

He looked up at the bright shape across the fields, then back down at the ditch. And up again, blinking to clear the rain from his eyes. He took a short pace forwards, then stepped back, whimpering quietly to himself. A small light wind drifted in from the right, blowing cold rain against his cheek. And Pork made up his mind.

The first two steps he took brought him to the edge of the slope leading down to the ditch. Again he hesitated, but only for a moment. And then with a scurrying rush he was down the slope and plunging head-first into the dank waters of the moat itself.

It was even deeper than it looked, and a foul-tasting slime filled the hedgehog's mouth and nostrils as he sank. He sank a very long way and by the time he managed to claw his way back up to the surface he was choking and gasping for air. His paws threshed at the water ahead of him and kicked out desperately behind him, but he couldn't stop himself going under again.

Now there was a rushing rumbling sound in his ears and red lights in his head. He swallowed a great throatful of water and spluttered loudly as he surfaced for the second time.

Somehow he managed to reach the bank and pull himself up the wet slope. And then he just lay there on the grass with the rain driving down on his back, wheezing and struggling for breath.

But he was a sturdy creature and before long he'd recovered and was standing up again, scanning the darkness for the gleaming shape.

It wasn't there. It was gone, and in its place was semi-darkness and nothing else. Pork frowned. He rubbed the ditchwater from his eyes and looked again, but it made no difference. He licked his mouth unhappily and went on staring out into the night.

It soon became clear that what he was looking at was not the wide acreage of ploughed fields. It was the forest itself. In his struggles with the dirty moat he'd somehow turned full-circle and found his way back to the same grassbank where the badgers had discovered him.

He groaned, then shot round and blinked at the darkness. The shining thing was still there, and he moved almost instinctively towards it. There was a strange little smile on his face and even the sight of the dark ditch staring back at him couldn't wipe it off. Down the slope he went, straight into the slimy waters and under them. And up again, blowing water through his nose. When he reached the other side his spines were clotted with mud and filth and there was more mud on his belly and legs. The wounds on his snout and ear were caked and staunched with the stuff, and he had brown slime in his mouth. He coughed it out, spat it away from him, and rubbed his eyes with two furry fists. The ludicrous leaf on his back was somehow still there.

A fat cloud drifted across the face of the moon. The wind died away. Pork looked up and saw that the bright thing was now less bright. He frowned again and set off towards it at once.

The fields were now just one vast quagmire and Pork's progress was slow. There were no furrows anymore. They'd all been obliterated by the rain and now there was nothing but mud. Mud that swamped Pork's little round body and made it even more brown than usual. And puddles that covered his short legs and belly when he splattered his way through them. And all the way across the mud, the rain went on sheeting down and the shiny object grew less and less bright.

Pork was nearly there and the moon had almost disappeared when he trod awkwardly on a hidden stone and broke his foreleg. He didn't know it was broken, but he squealed with the sudden pain and was forced to stop. He looked up, eyes watering, and saw that the bright shape was now rather pale.

The pain made his leg throb, but he dragged himself on across the mire, sobbing and nursing his leg, keeping his eyes fixed on the twisting shape. It was no longer very bright, but to slow Pork it was still a beautiful thing. And the thought of reaching it and being with it pushed him on over the last few muddy yards.

The clouds rolled over the moon and covered it, blotted it out. The hedgehog hauled himself through the bedraggled grass on the edge of the waterlogged field, and he was there, on the curving thing itself.

It was a road, of course. Hard and uncomfortable to touch. Pork stared at it in dismay, then lay down on his side and wept quietly into the fur of his shoulder. He didn't see the twin spots of light that punctured the darkness a long way off, and all he heard was the rain. But then the road began to tremble and he caught the sound of a distant rumbling. Cold, frightened, and in pain, he buried his nose deep into his belly for protection.

The rumbling noise grew louder. Then very loud. There was a faint squeak of turning rubber, a spasm of intense light. And then what had once been round Pork was just a flat patch of hedgehog, turning red in the rain and the moonless night.

M O N

H IGH IN A TREE, ON THE RIM OF A hollow, there was a brown owl with eyes wide open in the darkness. He was a thin brown owl, very old, with a rather pinched face, and his name was Mon.

The wind brushed across his body and the rain made his feathers wet, but the owl didn't mind. He gazed down at the road below and the mess of hedgehog in the middle of it.

Stupid things, he thought to himself. Hopeless stupid animals with not a scrap of common sense among them. Curling themselves into a useless little ball and getting crushed as a result. Learning the hard way is one thing, but this is madness. Stupid creatures.

He looked up and away. The rain was falling long and hard, bouncing off his rather flat head, dripping off his beak. And he ignored it.

Apart from the rain, there wasn't much to look at. Just the roof of the forest swaying in the wind, and the twisting road.

But it made no difference to Mon. He wasn't interested in sightseeing. He'd stepped out from the shelter of his hollow because he enjoyed the rain and because he was hungry.

Being such an old owl, he wasn't much good at hunting his own food anymore. His wings didn't work properly. And that was infuriating. He hated his old age. It was a despicable, inconvenient thing. Not so long ago, he would have swept down through the cold air, homing in on a field mouse or some unsuspecting rabbit, and crush it in his angry claws. He never missed, even when the night was at its darkest. He struck fast and decisively, without a sound, without giving it a second thought. Now he was too old.

And he was hungry. He hadn't eaten for some time and his stomach was making its usual complaints. He'd tried to keep the wretched thing quiet by swallowing large doses of rainwater, but it was no use. He had to have something to eat.

Old Mon was a proud owl, one of the proudest. But even he had to admit this was no time for things like pride. So he took a deep breath and rather reluctantly sent out a call for help, the long low unmistakeable hoot of the brown owl.

He took another breath and hooted again. Then he blinked once or twice in the rain and waited for something to happen.

Not too far away, a pair of black shapes were flying along the edge of the forest with the rain slanting across their faces. They were both owls, one male, one female, and they were on their way home. They were large birds, round and solid, and they said nothing together as they flew. They travelled side by side, the female owl staying closer to the forest. She was a little bigger than her companion, her plumage was more grey than brown, and her name was Hula. The other owl was shorter and slightly older, with a thickly muscled chest. His name was Brusk and he had a black beak.

They were still a long way from home when they first heard old Mon's hoot for help. Even through the driving rain they heard it quite clearly.

"I wonder who that is," said the female owl.

Her companion shrugged.

"Who cares?" he said.

"Well, whoever it is doesn't sound too happy."

Brusk grunted. Hula stared hard into the darkness.

"It came from those tall trees up ahead," she noted. "We really ought to know who lives up there."

"Well, we don't," said Brusk. And that was that. They flew on in silence for a while, with nothing but the rain for company. Another dismal hoot drifted across the night, but they ignored it. Then there was no noise except the downbeat of their wings and the pouring rain.

"It's no good," said Hula at last. "We can't just ignore it."

"Yes we can."

"No, Brusk. You know very well we can't."

"It's got nothing to do with us," he insisted.

She shook her head.

"It's someone who needs help, that's all I know. And we can't just fly past like this. You know that as well as I do."

He did too. It was the first law of owlish conduct. But

he was tired and wet and impatient to get home. He said nothing again and scowled at the trees.

"Well anyway," said Hula, "I'm going to see what's going on."

"Oh all right," said Brusk. "It's probably some old scrounger who wants to be fed. Drop a couple of mice in his den and then come home. I'll wait for you there."

"I won't be long," she smiled, brushing his wing with hers. Then she turned and veered away into the night.

Brusk watched her leave, then turned back to continue his flight.

It didn't take Hula long to find the tree she was looking for. There was an owl in it. A very old owl, very thin and ragged, with the rain soaking his droopy old feathers.

When he saw her flying towards him, old Mon didn't move a muscle. He didn't even seem to notice her. When she swooped down and alighted on the edge of the hollow, he didn't say anything. Nor did she. And they just stood like that for a while, each waiting for the other to speak first. From time to time he would turn his head slowly and look at her with one peppery old eye before turning back to stare at the treetops.

Hula found herself smiling at him. Not mockingly, but because he seemed such a proud old bird, standing there with so much stiff dignity in the rain. She felt she ought to say something nice to him.

"Well?"

It was all he said and he said it very crustily, but at least it was something. Hula was quite surprised to hear him speak at all.

"Well?" she echoed, wondering what he meant by it.

"Well?" said Mon, with even more vinegar in his voice. "Well, what's the problem, then? What do you want?"

She half-raised an eyebrow.

"I think I should be asking you that question," she said quietly.

He turned his head again and fixed her with that fiery old eye of his.

"Impertinent, eh?" he said slowly. "Left your manners back home, have you?"

"Not at all," she said calmly. "I was on my way home and I heard a call for help."

"Well, it wasn't me." And he turned his head away from her.

"Yes it was."

He turned his head back to her.

"What do you mean by that?"

She shrugged.

"It was you I heard hooting. That's what I mean."

He looked her full in the face and opened his beak. Then he shut it again and looked away without saying a word.

"Well?"

"Well what?" he said grouchily.

"Well, what can I do to help?"

"Nothing."

She smiled again.

"Are you ill?" she asked.

"No."

"What then?"

He shifted about on the rim of the hollow, lifted one leg, and gave himself a quick nervous scratch.

"Hungry," he said very quietly.

"What?" said Hula, leaning towards him slightly.

"Hungry, I said! Hungry! What's the matter? Deaf as well as saucy, are you?"

She lowered her voice a fraction.

"What do you prefer?" she said. "Mice or moles?"

"Mice," he said rather comically, without looking at her.

"Mice it is then." And she sprang up from the hollow in a flurry of wings. He didn't watch her fly away, but he looked altogether more perky as he waited for her to return.

The rain was as relentless and spiteful as ever. As he stood there, drenched to the skin, Mon picked up the first distant growls of thunder, far away to the north. He didn't mind that. He was fond of thunderstorms and he had no fear of lightning. He'd lived through it all before and he considered himself far too old to start worrying about things like that now.

The rumbles in his stomach brought him back to thinking about food, and about mice in particular. By now he was really quite famished, so he was very relieved to see the female owl sweeping in towards him through the gloom.

"There," she announced, as she deposited a bulbous little wood mouse across the threshold of the hollow. Mon's eyes lit up at the sight of it, but his manner was still abrupt.

"You'll have to cut it up for me," he said brusquely. "I can't swallow them as I used to."

"Of course," said Hula, and she set about the task.

"We'd better take it inside first," said Mon, and they dragged the carcass into the hollow.

Neither of them spoke as he was feeding—Mon because

his mouth was full, and Hula because she was busy watching him. She noticed above all that his eyes were brighter and everything about him was more urgent. He must have been really very hungry, she thought.

When the last morsel of mouse had disappeared, the old owl ran a damp wingtip across his beak and looked up at his visitor.

"Thank you," he muttered. It was the first friendly thing he'd said.

Hula was pleased.

"It's nothing," she said, predictably.

"On the contrary," said Mon. "It's the tastiest snack I've had for a long time."

She smiled.

"Yes," he went on, "I'm rather partial to a nice juicy little mouse. There's nothing quite like it as an appetiser."

"Appetiser?" she queried. "If you're still hungry I can fetch you another one."

"No no, my dear," said Mon quietly. "There's no need for that."

Then there was silence for a time. It was dry inside the hollow, and quieter. Hula found herself watching the trees tilting outside through the curtain of rain. It was good, she reflected, to be inside again, out of the storm. She felt much warmer and rather safe.

"I'm an old owl," said Mon quite suddenly.

She looked at him. How bright his eyes were.

"Yes," she said. "I know that."

He chuckled. It wasn't a pleasant sound.

"No, my dear. I'm very old. Ancient. Old as the hills and all that."

Hula frowned.

"I don't think I understand," she said.

"Of course not," said Mon, and he edged a little closer to her. "I wouldn't expect you to. But believe me, I'm older than you could ever imagine. Even the trees are younger than I am."

He's mad, thought Hula. She felt sorry for him, but at the same time she felt slightly uncomfortable. She decided to humour him.

"You don't look older than the trees," she said.

Mon frowned and his voice grew more serious.

"Oh, don't mock me, my dear. I'm not soft in the head, you can count on that. I know it sounds impossible but there it is. I'm the oldest of owls. The first owl."

"The first?" she said blankly.

"The very first. Now you can't get much older than that, can you?"

It was her turn to frown.

"The first owl," he went on. "Old as life itself. Old as death."

Hula was really rather disturbed by all this. It was clear that the old bird believed what he was saying—and the things he was saying were just not possible. And yet in a way it was hard not to believe him. She felt a faint shiver trickle down her neck.

"Old as death," he repeated, almost to himself. "That's me, my dear," he added with no fuss, as if he were telling her the time of year, "the Bird of Death."

She looked at him, at his little pinched face glowing pale and intense in the shadows. There was nothing friendly about him now. He looked every inch a bird of prey.

"I'm too old," he said. "Too weak to hunt for myself. Too frail to even leave this old tree. But I survive."

He looked hard at her, took a jerky step forward. She

edged backwards, felt her spine press against the wall of the hollow. She couldn't bring herself to look at his eyes.

"Even an ageless owl has to eat," he said, with a flicker of menace in his voice. "So I feed. On mice and dormice, on anything you fledglings can come up with. Not the most dignified existence for the Death Owl, I grant you, but it can't be helped. And I manage to vary my diet . . ."

Hula said nothing, and she was just thinking that he really was feeble-minded after all, when his voice grew suddenly louder and infinitely stronger.

"But you're not here to listen to an old owl's mutterings, are you, my dear? No, you're here to keep me fed."

She looked up sharply. She was aware that his fierce little body was now between her and the safety of the night outside. Then all she saw were a pair of little red eyes glinting in the blackness, and a tiny beak as harsh as death itself.

Before he went home, Brusk took time off to snatch a quick meal. When his ears caught the sound of a rustle in the undergrowth, he didn't hesitate. He fell upon the timid bank vole and trapped it with his claws, stifling its death-squeal in the speed of his attack. Then he swallowed it whole and went home.

Home for Hula and Brusk was a large gap in a cluster of broken trees and bushes in a corner of the forest. Nothing exotic, but warm and dry. He stayed here for some time, half-listening to the sounds of the storm, waiting for Hula to return. And when she didn't, he made up his mind to go back out and look for her. She could look after herself, he knew that. But on a night like this, it was better to make sure. Besides, he was bored.

He found the return journey longer and harder. The

wind had changed direction and was now blowing the rain straight into his face. But he pressed on, beating his wings and cursing under his breath.

From time to time he called out her name, but there was no answer, and it was pure chance that he happened to come across old Mon's tree. There was no reason to suspect that Hula was anywhere near this tall crumbling birch, but for a moment Brusk thought he heard sounds coming from the hollow near the top. And it looked a fairly likely place for an owl's den, so he flew straight towards it.

When he landed on the lip of the hole, he paused for a few seconds to shake some of the rain from his feathers and to clear his eyes by blinking. There was nothing much inside the thin hollow. Just a scrappy pile of rotten tree-bark, and an elderly owl.

"Well, old one," said Brusk, glancing casually around the hollow, "this isn't a bad place to spend the time."

"It keeps me dry," said Mon curtly.

Brusk nodded. He stopped looking around and looked at the owl instead. And the owl looked right back at him without flinching.

"I'm looking for my hen, old one. Has she passed this way?"

Mon's expression didn't change.

"No," was all he said.

"Well then," said Brusk, "it seems I'm in the wrong place."

"Yes."

Brusk looked back over his shoulder. The rain was still there. A thin strip of lightning appeared for half a second, far away in the night. Then a soft grumble of thunder. He was on the point of leaving, and he looked back inside for one last word to the old owl. Then he heard—or thought he heard—a kind of muffled whimper. Not much, just a hint of sound, but it was enough. He glanced down round behind Mon's skinny legs and caught sight of a heap of feathers, the crumpled body of another owl. With a gasp he realised it was the body of his companion.

"Hula!" he said hoarsely—but it was all he had time to say because at that moment old Mon moved with surprising speed and launched himself on his husky young visitor with all his weight.

Brusk fell backwards into space and in his surprise at being attacked he fell quite a long way before recovering. Flapping wildly, he righted himself at last and swept back upwards. He was angry now. Furious. And desperately anxious about his female. He flung himself hastily at the murderous old owl, who was now guarding the entrance to the hollow—but he'd completely underestimated Mon's strength and he was easily driven back. The rain washed the lines of blood from his cheek and chest.

"Go back," said Mon in a calm voice. "There's nothing for you here."

"You've got my hen in there," said Brusk breathlessly. "I won't leave without her."

"There's nothing you can do for her," said Mon. "She's food for me now."

"No!" cried the young owl, and he threw himself forward again, driving his claws into Mon's soft belly and tearing at him with his black beak. The old owl hissed with pain. For a moment he was forced back into the hollow, but there was timeless energy in his wiry old muscles and he defended himself skilfully, slicing his young enemy's face with his talons.

This time Brusk was very badly injured. Stunned and

bleeding freely from the head, he dropped from the hollow like a stone, the pain crackling in his ears. He managed to stop himself hitting the ground, but only just. Then he twisted painfully upwards and fluttered back to confront the passive figure of old Mon.

"Go back," said the old cannibal. "You're fighting something you can't understand."

At that moment there was a hint of movement behind Mon's back. It was Hula. As her senses returned, she felt the stinging pains across her body where Mon had used his beak and claws, and her ears picked up a confusion of sounds: the rain, the clamour of fighting owls, and above all that, two familiar voices. She looked up, wiped the blood from her eye. She saw the black outline of her attacker blocking the entrance to the hollow, and beyond him the ragged flapping shape of her wounded companion.

"Brusk," she murmured, but she was too weak to be heard. She could see, however, that Brusk was badly hurt, and despite her weakness she knew what she had to do. It all happened very quickly. She struggled to her feet, ruffled her wings, and thrust herself against the aged body of the killer owl.

It was enough—just enough—to nudge him off the ledge and away from the tree, enough to send him fluttering out into the open with a loud squawk. And now old Mon felt the pangs of fear for the first time. Real fear, fear of falling to the ground where he'd be immobilised and helpless, where even his great strength would not be enough to keep him alive forever. He beat the air with his fragile wings and managed to scramble back to the sanctuary of his ledge. He swung round at once, but it was too late. Hula was gone. He turned, and was just in time to see the two young owls helping each other to wend their way over the dark treetops, injured but out of reach.

And it was all over. They had escaped, and for a moment Mon was viciously angry. But the anger died away. He knew it didn't really matter. Others had escaped before, others had lived to tell the tale. And others would pass his way again. Old Mon would just wait for them, call them towards him out of the sky with a few shrewd hoots. While he was alone, on the rim of his bare hollow in the darkness and the rain, he was just another rather scrawny old owl with thin blood and mournful eyes. But he would wait, as he'd waited for hundreds of years—and he would always be there, in his tall tree, silent and eternally patient, as the Death Owl should be.

RUSALKA

SOMEWHERE IN A WARM AND SWEATING summer night, there was a sycamore tree with no branches. At the foot of the sycamore, surrounded by forest, was the thin crouching figure of a grey squirrel.

He was young and dirty, restless, with a face like a rat—and a closer look would have revealed that he was the very same squirrel who'd come across Pork the hedge-hog among the beech trees.

But that had been a long time ago and now the squirrel was alone and indulging himself in his favourite pastime of doing nothing in the undergrowth. After a while he got up and went for a walk.

He found himself on a narrow forest path and it was warm and wet under his feet. He saw the moon. It was off-white and watery and since he had nothing better to do, he looked at it. But it was only the moon after all, and soon he turned away and went on walking along the path.

It was a quiet night, with nothing but the sound of creaking trees. But it was an itching kind of quiet, and the young squirrel's nose twitched as he walked. It was a different night, even though everything seemed the same as usual. He stopped for a moment and scratched the side of his neck, listening very hard and smelling the air. And then he looked up for no reason and saw something that choked the breath in his throat.

From the tangle of branches halfway up a group of skinny trees, there emerged a single black stump edged with moonlight. And on the stump was the silhouette of the most beautiful red squirrel he'd ever seen. He could tell she was a red squirrel because she had tufted ears, and he knew she was beautiful—he just knew it. He didn't speak, just stood there half-crouching on the path with his eyes bright and his nose quivering. He took a couple of hesitant steps forward.

Then she was gone. Just like that. Gone, leaving the branches and the moon behind her. And the breathless grey squirrel on the forest lane. And the echoes of her strange laughter vanishing among the trees.

It was daytime again and the morning sun took its time getting to mid-day as the forest sweltered beneath it. Somewhere in the bracken, an old dog-fox scratched itself and picked its teeth after breakfast. A pair of badgers slept fitfully in their set, snoring in the dust. A family of bad-tempered woodlarks squabbled in their nest under the roots of a tree. And a puny grey squirrel spent the whole day wandering about the forest without getting tired. He seemed to have no need of food or water and his eyes were always feverishly bright. He spoke to no-one, feared nothing. And all he did was scurry about from tree to tree, looking in every hollow. Every so often he was chased away by an irate squirrel or a gloomy pair of owls. He managed to disturb half the forest without knowing it. Towards the end of the day, he was trudging along a ridge of drying grass.

"Hello rat-face!" a passing jackdaw called out merrily. He ignored it. His ugliness was something he'd learned to live with a long time ago, and he had other things on his mind. After a while he stopped. Not because he was tired but because there was no point going any further. There was nothing for him to do, so he simply stayed where he was, waiting impatiently for the night.

"Ah, Reek," said a friendly voice. "I thought it was you."

He looked up, recognising the familiar roguish accent of his favourite grand-uncle.

"What's the matter then—bitten your tongue off?"

"No, uncle."

"No? Well, you'd better use it then. What's the matter, I said."

"Nothing, uncle."

The old squirrel raised a bushy eyebrow.

"Oh, I see," he said simply. "A female."

"No!" said Reek hurriedly, but his uncle just laughed.

"Liar!" he said cheerfully.

Reek looked at him and couldn't help smiling.

"I'm all right, uncle," he said. "Really I am."

"All right, are you? I wouldn't say that. You're an ugly little specimen, for a start."

"Uncle!"

"And a sulky one too, come to think of it. Just because some pesky female's got under your skin—"

"It's not true, uncle!"

"It is true, uncle," said the old squirrel. "It's only a female, you know," he added kindly.

Reek's head reared up.

"Oh, she's not—she's beautiful!"

"I don't doubt it," said his uncle. "They always are."

"But really—she's perfect."

"Yes, and they're always perfect too."

"Oh, you're impossible!" snorted Reek.

"True enough," said the old squirrel. "But you've got to keep a sense of proportion, see? Keep smiling and all that."

Reek smiled.

"I know, uncle. But it's not that easy."

"Well of course it's not easy! Wouldn't be the same if it was easy. What do you expect, eh? It's not a game of tag, you know."

Reek laughed, and his uncle wrapped a grizzly old arm around his shoulders.

"Take my advice, ugly one," he said confidentially. "Forget her. And if you can't forget her, tread carefully."

Reek sighed impatiently.

"That's just what everyone else has been telling me," he lied.

"That's just what I've been telling you too," said his uncle. "Which means it's worth bearing in mind, see? Tread carefully. That's a fine piece of advice, let me tell you. So make sure you ignore it."

The young squirrel frowned.

"Now you're confusing me," he said.

"Ignore it, I say. Learn the hard way. It's always the best way to learn. Besides," he added, with a monstrous wink of his eye, "the hard way's so much more fun!"

Reek laughed and the old squirrel left him like that, laughing. Reek watched him amble off into the trees, then went off. He turned and went off to do nothing somewhere else.

And then, gradually, it was night again. As the clouds dozed across the moon, Reek the squirrel stopped for a rest. He clambered up onto the first branch of an old birch tree and stayed there for a time with his head against the treetrunk and his paws in his lap. He felt the day's fatigue spreading over him and let it lull him to sleep as he breathed in the heat and the warm night wind.

He had no idea why he woke up, but when he did he watched the moonlight spattering its shadows along the branch of his tree. The air was still warm, but he didn't notice it. He felt strangely sick.

Then he saw her. She was right at the end of his branch, framed by hanging twigs with the moon in the background. And it was her—there was no doubt about that. He felt the same twisting pain in his belly and he'd stopped breathing again. Then she laughed. Just once, the same wild laugh he remembered from the previous night. It frightened him like nothing else, that laugh—but he couldn't stop himself creeping closer to her along the branch.

She was gone again. Simply not there in the night. And Reek could hardly believe it.

"Oh no!" he cried, and it came out as a squeal. "No, don't go. I won't hurt you."

But there was no answer. There was no sound at all.

"Don't go," he said softly. He felt the first tears on the edge of his eyes as he stared hopelessly into the darkness. There really was nothing there. Just the night and the dull throb of his own pulse. He bowed his head and let the tears soak themselves into his thin little cheeks as he cried till his head ached and he was too exhausted to keep awake. Then he fell asleep.

When Reek woke up he felt terrible. His mouth was dry and his body ached all over. There was thick sleep in his eyes so he rubbed them and got up.

The rest of the day came and went and yet again he did nothing except wait for the night to appear. When it was dark he went looking for his red squirrel and this time he couldn't find her. Then he went to sleep.

The next night it was the same story. The waiting, the darkness, and no sign of her. It went on like that for weeks: night after night, day after restless day. And the ugly little squirrel did nothing but go on searching. He ate very little and hardly ever slept. He lost all track of time, lost touch with his family, and talked to no-one but himself.

After a while, the lack of food and sleep caught up with him and he started to see things that weren't there. Especially in the night, when the moon and shadows played tricks with his vision. Often he thought he saw the red squirrel herself somewhere in the distance. But she was never there, and before long he was too weak to worry anymore. He stopped looking for her and started quietly wasting away, muttering to himself under the roots of a horse chestnut tree.

And then one night a high wind was blowing. It came from nowhere in particular and it was sudden, hot, and dry. It flustered the undergrowth and dragged the carpet of leaves on the forest floor behind it. And it didn't go away.

Reek the squirrel felt the wind in his face and slowly opened his eyes. He didn't look at anything and he found it hard to breathe, but he sniffed once or twice before closing his eyes again.

Then he heard the voice of the red squirrel laughing in the storm. He ignored it at first, thinking it was just another trick of the night, but then he heard it again. It was coming from somewhere in the tree above him and he turned his face upwards. Then it was coming from somewhere behind him.

He jumped up and stood looking around him, squinting in the wind. His head was spinning and there was no strength in his legs but he didn't care. He hopped round the tree and looked behind it. He hopped back again and peered into the bushes on the left. And still nothing.

Then he heard her laughter right behind him and he leapt sideways with half a shriek, tripped over a fat root, and ended up on his back at the base of a tree, breathing hard and wiping a rancid leaf from his nose.

He looked up. She was there. He caught his breath. And then, of course, she laughed. It was more of a chuckle than a laugh, a low rustle from deep in her throat. Reek tried to speak but couldn't. It was all he could do to keep himself from running away. And then instead of laughing she said something.

"Hello." It wasn't much, just the usual greeting, but Reek thought it was a lovely sound, warm and earthy and just a little eerie. He tried to say hello too, but all he could come up with was a kind of hoarse squeak.

She smiled, but not unkindly.

"What's your name?" she asked.

He fiddled nervously with his fingers.

"Reek," he said.

"Reek?" she laughed. "What a silly name that is."

The way she said it made it seem the best thing anyone had ever said to him. He couldn't think of anything to say in return, but he thought he ought to smile or something. So he did, squeezing out a thin, rather awkward little smirk. His nose twitched.

She moved a little closer.

"Don't you want to know my name?" she asked.

He did, very much. He nodded gawkily at her.

"Yes," he squeaked. Then he corrected himself. "Yes," he said again, in something like his normal voice.

"Rusalka," she said, rolling her tongue around the word. She seemed to enjoy the name as much as he did.

And then he saw her moving away.

"No!" he cried, leaping to his feet. She didn't speak but he could see that she was still there, standing quite still in the darkness.

"I want to see you again," he said.

She laughed, and the laugh died in the fierce wind.

"And you will," she said.

"When?"

"Tomorrow. In the night."

"Where?"

Again that wild maddening laugh. The jumping wind-swept leaves hid her from view as she slipped away into the blackness, but the laughter was still there. That and her last words.

"I will find you, Reek," she sang. "I will find you."

———

And she did. Not just that night but the one after that. And every night from then on, as the summer burnt itself out into autumn.

They were delicious nights for Reek the squirrel. At first he would often wonder how his new companion could possibly choose to waste her time with anyone as supremely ugly as himself. But he soon stopped worrying about it and instead lost himself in the deep pleasures of simply being with her. She was very much, he thought, like some kind of rich scented fruit. He'd never known anything like her voice, or the touch and smell of her fur. No-one had ever bothered to talk to him as she did, and he spent most of the long nights just listening and smiling all over his face.

And at the end of each of these nights she left him. Every time. She was always back when the night returned, but he never saw her when it was light.

"Why not?" he asked her.

They were nestled together in a low hollow halfway up a tree. She stroked his cheek with her paw.

"Does it matter?" she asked.

"Oh no," he said quickly. "No, I was just wondering, that's all."

"Well, it's not important," she assured him. Her nose touched his for a moment and he smiled in the darkness. Then they lay back in the warmth of the hollow and basked in the next silence.

But in the empty days that followed, Reek found himself giving the matter further thought. Perhaps Rusalka simply didn't like to see him in the daylight, knowing how hideous he was. But he was sure there was more to it than that. She was, after all, a very strange animal. Even after all this time she was still a mystery to him, still vaguely frightening. Like some kind of beautiful witch. And he knew nothing of her past, or where she lived, or anything like that.

After many days spent in thoughts like these, his curiosity got the better of him. One night, when there was no moon or wind, he watched her leaving him as usual, gliding away across the forest. When she was almost out of sight he started to follow her, running silently from one tree to the next and breathing very softly.

Ahead of him, Rusalka didn't stop. She moved quickly, relentlessly, so that Reek had trouble keeping up with her. Once or twice he thought he'd lost her completely, but he never quite did. Then the dawn came up and everything was half-light. A few morning birds began to chatter. And the red she-squirrel came to a halt.

Watching from behind a greasy oak-root, Reek saw her jump up onto a sort of ledge formed by the interlocking branches of a pair of stunted poplar trees. He saw her dark little body scoot up the side of one of the poplars, flying up the mossy trunk. Then she was gone, and he stepped out from his hiding-place.

He was already on his way up the treetrunk when for some reason he stopped. Nothing had happened, there was nothing in his way, he didn't know exactly why he'd hesitated. But something wasn't right. It was there in the air around him, the same vague shiver he'd felt just before his first-ever glimpse of the red squirrel. He sniffed and glanced around for a moment. Then he took a quick deep breath and scurried further up the treetrunk.

Near the top of the poplar, partly obscured by hanging scraps of bark, there was a small crooked cleft. Reek looked at it, looked around it, then squeezed his way in.

He was in a hollow, a dry and gloomy little den with

nothing in it, and he frowned. There was no sign of the she-squirrel, even though he knew she wasn't far away. He decided to go out and look somewhere else—and then a dark slim chasm in the far side of the hollow caught his eye.

It was only just wide enough to accommodate his eager little body and he had to struggle along it, clambering upwards in a long spiral. When the narrow passage came to an end he found himself squatting tentatively at the entrance of another, wider tree-chamber.

There was a ragged curtain of green straw across the mouth of it, and from behind the curtain, sounds of movement. So he knew she was there. But he didn't know what to do next. He felt the blood pushing through his head, and his breathing sounded far too loud. He wanted to run away once and for all, but he didn't. He couldn't. So he took a huge breath, nudged his way through the straw curtain—and she was there, with her back to him.

He didn't say anything but she heard him come in and turned to face him, jumping like a demon. And when Reek saw her face, he couldn't believe it.

He found himself staring at the roughest, most raw-boned, most profoundly ugly squirrel's face he'd ever seen. She was almost impossibly ugly and Reek could hardly bear to keep on looking at her. But he did, staring quietly with his mouth slack and half-open.

She took one look at him, saw who he was, then leapt away to the far corner of the hollow and stayed there with her back to him, hiding her face in her paws and sobbing vigorously in the shadows.

Reek still said nothing. But then there was really nothing much to say. There was no sorcery here, no strange animal nightmares, no reason to be afraid. Just a filthy-ugly red she-squirrel in a tree. He turned and walked out.

Outside, it was warm and quite bright. The sun and the sky. Some of the forest. A day like all the others, in fact. He stood there and looked at it all, pouting as he did so. And thinking. Then he went back in through the thin hole in the tree.

She was still there, crying quietly in the corner. When he put his paw on her neck, her body stiffened and she stopped sobbing, but she didn't say anything and she didn't look up. He couldn't see her face, huddled as it was in her paws, but he could smell her moist body-scent and he felt the lush fur under his fingers. None of that had changed. And he knew he'd been right to come back.

"Now I'll be able to see you in the daytime too," he said very softly.

She lifted her head but kept her paws on her cheeks. Her eyes were large and bloodshot.

"You've seen how I am," she said in a small voice.

"Yes," he agreed.

She took her paws away from her face. He didn't flinch.

"Why are you back?" she asked.

"Well," said Reek, rather slowly, "I'm no woodland rose myself, am I?"

She didn't argue. Instead she took his paw and led him out into the daylight. In the folds of a nearby maple tree, a rascally old grey squirrel watched as they came out, laughed with them and nodded his head in approval, though they never saw him do it.

N A

THE STACK OF OLD LOGS IN ONE
corner of the clearing had been there for years. The
logs were green and brown and very wet. A last layer of
snow melted on top of them. From a gap between two
of the logs near the bottom, a pair of eyes were watching.

The eyes were more red than brown and they were
looking out across the snow-spattered clearing, following
with particular interest the movements of a large carrion
crow as it picked its way from one patch of grass to another.

It had been a hard winter for the crow. The freezing
cold had obligingly killed a whole feast of small animals
and birds, but the snow had covered many of their bodies
—so the crow had been forced to wander far from its
usual haunts in search of food. Now it found itself pecking
about in this miserable little clearing, scratching at the late

morning grass with its stiff black claws and losing its temper.

When it heard a slight noise near the stack of logs, its first reaction was one of hopeful surprise. It turned and looked round, half expecting to spot a wood mouse or some small injured bird trying to creep past unnoticed. But what it saw was something altogether different. Emerging from the gap at the base of the log-pile, its eyes firmly fixed on the crow's lean black body, was a stoat.

In winters gone by, when it had been desperate with hunger, the crow had fought and killed a number of animals as large as itself. But a stoat—well, that was a different matter. And the one that was easing itself out from between the logs looked a particularly nasty piece of work. For a start, it was very big. Almost twice the size of a regular stoat. It was darker too, and its fur was long and coarse. There was clearly more than a drop of polecat blood in its veins. The crow took one look at its dark red eyes and the spittle around its mouth—and decided it was time to leave. It spread its wings to fly away.

Then, out of the corner of its eye, it saw the stoat moving away to the left, holding one of its paws high in the air. Intrigued by this, the crow put its wings down and turned its head to get a better view. As it did so, the stoat promptly fell over and lay still, on its side in a puddle of slush.

So that's it, thought the crow. The bastard's pretending to be injured. Well I'm not falling for that. But then the stoat sprang to its feet and turned a cartwheel, landing flat on its face. After that it got up and chased its tail in circles. The crow watched all this with wide eyes. It had never seen an insane stoat before. It was so mesmerised by the animal's antics that it forgot all its fear and wariness.

And all the time, the stoat was working its way closer and closer with every jump and somersault.

Then it was close enough. It turned its back on the crow for a moment—and the careless bird stepped up to see what it was doing. The stoat whipped round, grinning from ear to ear. It was only then, with its life on the sharp point of danger, that the starving crow realised what had been going on. It made an instant frantic attempt to escape, but it knew it had no chance. Even as it lifted its wings, the stoat sprang forward, reaching out with its claws. The soaking wet ground hindered its take-off and it slipped, giving the crow that extra half-second in which to get away. It lashed out with its wings and urged itself into the air—but not fast enough. Just as its feet left the ground, it felt the stoat's paw shoot out and grab one of its struggling wings.

Now the crow knew this was the end of everything. There was nothing left but to hope for a quick and painless death.

But even in this it was unlucky. The stoat aimed its death-bite at the back of the crow's thin black neck, but in its haste it missed completely and tore a great chunk out of the bird's shoulder, biting the muscle in half. The crow let out a dry high-pitched croak and tried to jerk away along the grass. But its wing was trapped under the stoat's paw and it couldn't move.

Instead of finishing the crow off, the stoat contented itself with bursting one of its eyes and lacerating the left side of its face with one swipe of its claws. Then it proceeded to drag the skinny black body across the clearing towards the stack of logs.

All this time, the stoat had said nothing. Not a word, not so much as a snarl. Once inside his own private little den, enclosed by the logs, he threw back his head and laughed, hissing happily to himself while the crow twitched in agony on the ground. Then he began his meal, scratching thin slivers of raw skin from the crow's ribs, gnawing at the sparse flesh on its legs and chest. The tortured bird shivered once or twice, but it had no strength left to cry out. And the stoat carried on eating, rolling the crow's body over and pulling one of its legs off. The sweet taste of blood freshened his mouth, and he savoured every loose drop of it.

It was his first meal for a long time, and not one of the best. But it was food, after all. And all food was good food. It was something the stoat had believed since the day he'd killed and eaten his mother. All food is good food and the next meal is the best.

When he was no longer hungry he left the crow's body alone and stood still for a while, thinking about what to do next. He licked his teeth. The taste of blood in the mouth, the smell of blood in the air—these were the exciting things. The stoat grinned and pissed contentedly in the dirt. Then he slipped out of his wooden hideout and disappeared under the drape of ferns across the clearing, leaving the carcass of the dying crow to go on itching and pulsing for a few minutes after he was gone.

While the stoat was just finishing his lunch, a late breakfast was being eaten in another part of the forest. A place where the trees were taller and more powerfully built, the undergrowth thicker, the soil (even in winter) always damp and fat like dark clotted cream, the whole place watered by the broad and languid river that lay across the belly of the forest.

Into the main river ran a network of smaller, more

urgent streams, each one lined with thinner trees and meagre hedgerows. One of these streams was a little wider and slower than the rest, and the fish that breathed in it were also a fraction wider and slower than most.

Moving steadily downstream was a whole flotilla of these fish. They were all roach, mostly young and bright green, and they were all hungry, as they had been all winter. So they drifted in and out of the long dangling weeds by the riverbank, nosing about for molluscs and stray insects.

The oldest of these fish was also the most tight-lipped. He had the biggest hump on his back and he appeared to be in charge of the others, though he said very little.

The old fish wasn't happy. The water didn't feel right. He knew this dozing stretch of river like one of his own fins, and he knew when it was on his side. He moved cautiously between the dark weeds. They were too closely packed for his liking. Things could hide amongst them.

He looked around at the rest of his shoal. They were having their breakfast now, most of them. Making do with weed leaves. The old fish watched them. They were all quite unconcerned, but he knew he was right to worry.

Then, as part of his routine, he counted them. There were two missing. His eyes opened wide and he counted again. There was no mistake.

The old roach didn't panic. He moved smoothly in amongst the others and collected them all together.

"What's all this then?" said one of his grandsons.

"Nothing," he said calmly. "Just time to move on, that's all."

The young fish shrugged and blew a few bubbles before joining the rest of the shoal. The old grandfather fish got them all into line and moved them off, away from the dense weeds towards the more open waters. None of them argued or complained about being dragged away from the feeding-grounds. They knew the old skipper was nearly always right.

The shoal began to move a little faster, keeping the weaker fish together in the middle of the column. Their leader glanced around him, searching the darkest corners with his eyes. Then he felt the water move behind him. Just the faintest shudder, but he felt it all the same. When he looked round he saw that another fish had disappeared.

He turned to tell the others it was time to swim even faster—then something caught his eye. He was too slow to see exactly what it was, but another roach was missing. He moved to the back of the fleet and stayed there.

"Move!" he cried, and his voice blasted through the water. "Move away—there's danger here! Move fast, all of you!"

And they did, all of them, their tail fins driving them on. The old fish raced along behind them, urging them to greater efforts. Still there was no sign of anything. He glanced to the left—and his whole face went suddenly slack with terror.

It came bursting out from the thin reeds near the river-bank, all mouth and huge staring eyes. The old roach knew at once what it was. There was no mistaking the face of the Horror Fish. He caught one brief glimpse of its white back-slanting teeth—then the monstrous killer pike lunged and swallowed him all in one movement.

So the old fish never saw the massacre which followed. Now that it was out in the open, the pike had no need or time for subtleties. Its great slouching mouth was every-where, swallowing most of the roach and butchering the rest, cutting them in half. The little fish dashed away in every direction, crazy with fear. But there was no way out, nowhere to hide from that bulging mouth. They all died, sooner or later. And even then the pike's hunger wasn't appeased. It snapped up the severed head of one of the smaller roach, then went on its way, sliding along the flank of the stream with a sleazy grin on its mouth and no expression in its eyes. Behind it, a few pieces of raw fish floated up to the surface. And a little blood. Something for the birds to pick at.

The stoat spent the afternoon roaming a section of the forest looking for something to kill. The cold and the snow were still keeping most animals indoors, so he was forced to go underground in search of his prey. But most of the places he visited were empty. All except one, and that had a family of rather large badgers in it. He left them well alone.

It was nearly evening when he arrived at the mouth of a small burrow in a steep bank of earth, and he was not in a good mood. He was even more annoyed when he discovered that the burrow was a very narrow one. It was a tight fit for the stoat. The walls of the tunnel pressed hard against his body as he struggled along it. Small blocks of soil crumbled down from the ceiling when he scraped his head on it, and his eyes and mouth were always filling with dirt. He spat the stuff out, sneezing and yapping to himself as he went.

Eventually, when his patience was at a very low ebb, he found himself scrambling out of the end of the tunnel into a large circular chamber. There were moles in it. Old Gaffer with his daughter and grandchildren, soft and silent in the darkness.

The old mole turned round. His heart sank. Even when

he was young his eyesight had been nothing special. Now, in his later years, it had become quite appallingly bad. But his sense of smell was still excellent, and it only needed one or two short sniffs to tell him that he and his little ones were in great danger.

He couldn't be sure what the animal in front of him was, but it smelt terrible. Like a polecat. It was big enough to be a polecat, too. And yet it was more like a stoat. Or a weasel. He could never tell the damned things apart. But whichever it was, old Gaffer knew it was something he couldn't fight. And trying to run away would be just as futile. Their only chance was to bluff it out.

He worked all this out very quickly. Then he shuffled forward and placed his bulky little body between his offspring and the stoat. He squinted up at the intruder's face and squared his shoulders.

"You, sir!" he boomed, in a voice that was almost steady. "Who are you and what can I do for you?"

The stoat frowned. He wasn't used to greetings of this sort.

"What's the matter?" bellowed the old mole. "Can't you hear me? I said, what's your name?"

The stoat's eyes narrowed.

"Na!" he said, spitting the word out like a piece of gristle.

"What's that?" yelled Gaffer. "Speak up, can't you? No-one's going to bite your head off."

"Na!" snapped the stoat. It was the only word he knew.

"Ah, I see," said the mole. "Well now, Mister Na, suppose you tell us what it is you want and we'll see what we can do to help."

But even as he finished speaking he knew it wasn't working. He sensed the stoat's muscles starting to tighten, heard it take a deeper breath. But still the old mole went on playing for time.

"Well, Mister Na, what do you say to that?"

The stoat took no notice of him. Behind the mole, his daughter was quietly nudging her children towards the safety of a small bolt-hole at the back of the earth-chamber. Na saw them moving and his frown turned into a leer. Old Gaffer sensed that too. He knew the stoat was about to strike, and he acted almost without thinking.

"Get out of here, you filth!" he roared. "No-one invited you in the first place. Get out at once!"

Again Na hesitated. He even took half a step backwards, and he looked at the fearsome old mole without knowing what to think. Gaffer knew he held the upper hand for a moment and he tried to keep the stoat's mind from settling by bombarding it with words.

"I know your sort," he sneered. "I'll bet you keep your own dung lying around outside your living quarters. Well, we don't want your sort round here. Do you hear me? Get out of here this minute!"

"Na!" said the stoat. "Na-na!" Then he sprang forward with a snarl on his face. The mole put up one of his broad pink hands, but it was only a token gesture and the stoat brushed it aside before burying his teeth in the back of Gaffer's skull. It was a bite that would have stunned a younger mole, but it killed old Gaffer where he stood. And Na turned to look for the daughter and her babies.

The three infant moles were almost at the mouth of the bolt-hole, with their mother behind them. She heard the stoat coming and turned to face him, blocking his path to her pups. But Na simply ripped half her face away with one bite and tore the velvet skin from her neck with his claws. Then he kicked her body aside and towered over the baby moles as they huddled in the shadows, whimpering with fear. He smiled at them and bared his teeth. Then he appeared to change his mind and turned away.

But before he left, he swung round and broke the spines of the first two youngsters with the weight of his paws. The last little mole was left alive, blinded and bleeding in the corner, while the stoat went outside to go and look for frogs, leaving old Gaffer's family to lie in the dirt, uneaten.

Vim the vole was basically a cheerful little soul, but not today. And he didn't know why. He crouched on the snow-covered bank of a small quiet river and looked anxious. Then he wiped his face with his paws and looked at the river. It was the same as it always was in winter: the bottle-green water dappled by the light glancing through the branches of a dozen willow trees; the glossy frozen mud on each bank; a few reeds standing idle in scattered groups; the snow. Vim loved the place. He would never have considered living anywhere else. But today even his old river frightened him.

He was cold, too. And hungry. And he knew that he would have to cross the river to get at his store of food on the far side. Frightened or not, he still had to eat. So he got up off his haunches and scurried down the bank. When he was at the water's edge he stopped and looked around, glancing unhappily up and down the river. Then he dropped into the water with a quick quiet splash and was soon paddling briskly towards the other side.

He kept looking round as he swam, and his breathing was very quick and very nervous. Every once in a while he dipped under the surface to see what was going on down there. One or two of the fish he saw were rather too large for his peace of mind, but none of them were carnivorous, and everything else seemed as quiet and docile as ever.

He was about halfway there, moving diagonally across the river, when he heard something behind him. Instead of hurrying on to the other side, he slowed down like a fool and looked back over his shoulder. There was a big dark stoat on the riverbank, its paws hidden in the thin rug of snow. And it had seen him.

Oh no, thought Vim. That's all I needed! He managed to look calm enough, but he was really quite petrified. He'd heard about this large hybrid beast before. He knew it was feared and hated more than any other animal— more than foxes or badgers, more than even the gang of rats who infested the riverbanks in summer. And he knew it could swim. There's no way out now, Vim old son, he told himself. You've had it.

Na thought so too. There were no bullfrogs for him to chase, but his eyes lit up at the sight of this poor defence-less little vole struggling across the river. And he laughed. Vim heard him and swam off as fast as he could—but the stoat was just as quick. He scrambled down the riverbank and set off in pursuit, ploughing through the water with his hefty forelegs.

Soon he was very close to the vole. Then he was closer still. He made a hasty stabbing lunge but he was still too far away. So he swam harder. He lunged again and his nose flicked against Vim's tiny rump. The water vole shrieked with terror, and Na laughed out loud.

"Na!" he said excitedly. "Na! Na-na!"

Then there was a loud disturbance in the water, away to the right. Na frowned and glanced sideways. He couldn't see anything, so he turned back to continue the chase.

But then the water was alive again and he stopped swimming to have a closer look.

It seemed that the whole river was in turmoil. It was swilling water against both its banks and there were volleys of large bubbles rolling on the surface, in a line down the middle. Na didn't like the look of it at all.

"Na," he muttered, and he sounded confused, perhaps even worried. He'd forgotten all about the water vole.

Then the water itself reared up angrily beside him and something struck him, tearing into his hip. The huge stoat screamed in pain. He doubled up, spluttering as the water swept into his nose and mouth. He couldn't feel his back leg.

"Na!" he cried. "Na! Na!"

Again the water exploded beside him, and this time he caught a glimpse of the olive-green back and dorsal fin of the vast killer pike as it lurched out from the weeds and bit another great hole in his body.

The lashing pain brought another scream from the stoat —but it also made him spit with anger. As the massive fish retreated, he struck out with his front foot. He felt something take the weight of his claws and he struck out again. And again after that. The pike's head broke the surface and Na saw the vacant grin on its face. There was a wound on its broad mottled back. It was his wound, he had put it there! And he laughed, shrieked with glee at the thought of it. Even when the pike crashed its teeth into him again he went on laughing. Laughing like something demented and biting at the demon fish with his own savage teeth.

But soon it was all finished. The water was calm again and tinselled with dark blood. On the far bank Vim the vole squatted on a clump of snow-wet grass and laughed all by himself, wringing his hands in relief and watching as the fragmented bodies of the two giant predators floated off together, very slowly, down the small river . . . the polecat-stoat with an eye hanging loose and his teeth in the air, laughing even in death . . . and large lumps of cold fish, white and green and bloodless. Something else for the birds to pick at.

REDGE

THE GREAT FOREST RIVER FELL DOWN
a waterfall, then strolled to the sea. To a wide cove
ringed by a solid wall of cliffs. And waves spattering against
black rocks in the sand.

Before the river reached the sea itself, it changed into a
saltwater inlet which in turn spread out into the wide cove.
On either side of the inlet, the land rose up in the form of
another wall of cliffs, and the last of the forest trees strag-
gled along the top edge of these cliffs like hairs standing
on end along a dog's back.

At the base of these bare limestone walls there were
several small caves with rock pools and sea shells in them.
And it was here, to one of these caves, that Redge the bat
came to spend a month or two every summer.

Redge was a whiskered bat, so he was very small and
brown. And old. Somewhere between middle age and
death. He usually came down to the sea with his female,

the one he called Number Two. But this summer he was alone.

He spent each day doing very little. Just hanging upside-down from the ceiling of his favourite cave, having a snooze. At night he'd wake up and go looking for insects to eat. Then it was back to the cave and another sleep. Not very adventurous, but it was all right for Redge. He was fond of the quiet life.

One day, late in the evening, he woke up as usual and stretched his legs, flexing his very long arms and shaking the stiffness out of his joints. He yawned once or twice and cleaned his ear with his thumb. Then he stopped and listened, keeping very still. There was someone else in the cave.

He could hear it very clearly, splashing about in one of the small shallow pools in the floor of the cavern. He looked down, but all he could see was a vague shape. He sent out a couple of fact-finding squeaks, very high in pitch, and the echoes of each squeak came bouncing back up through the semi-darkness. He could tell it was a large low-backed creature, but that was all. So he waited and watched, and did nothing.

Then he saw the creature stop paddling about in the rock pool. It stepped out of the water and shook itself. It looked up, and Redge guessed it was an otter. It seemed to be looking straight at him, but the bat was sure it couldn't see him, not at this range.

Then the otter took him completely by surprise.

"Redge?" it said enquiringly. "Is that you, Redge? Are you up there?"

Redge said nothing. He had no wish to advertise his presence until he knew who the newcomer was. And anyway, how did it know his name?

"Redge, it's me," it went on. "I'm not going to eat you. It's me, Redge. It's Kayak."

The bat opened his eyes very wide and peered hard at the otter's upturned face. It certainly didn't look unlike his old friend Kayak, and the voice was much the same. But it had been a long time and he couldn't be sure.

"Come on, Redge, stop messing about. It's me, I tell you. Are you up there?"

"No," said the bat, in his curious low-pitched voice.

"Well, why didn't you say so in the first place?" The otter's voice was cheerful and rustic, very broad and lusty. The voice of an active beast.

"Do you have to shout like that?" gruffed the bat. "You've got a voice like a fox's fart."

The otter guffawed with laughter.

"Still the same old Redge. You haven't changed a bit, have you?"

"Nor have you," said Redge. "You're still as loud and boring as ever." He sounded dry and caustic but his face was smiling. He was glad to see the otter.

"Anyway, you old grumbler," said Kayak, "why don't you come down here so we can have a civilised conversation? I'm getting a stiff neck looking up at you all the time."

"I can't," said Redge, and he flexed his fingers. "I can't fly. Chronic stiffness in my finger joints. I'll have to wait till it clears up."

"Ah, I see," said Kayak, nodding in sympathy. "That's very nasty, that is. Hope it gets better soon."

"Never mind that," said the bat. "How did you know I was up here in the first place?"

"Ah," said the otter knowingly. "That's easy. I didn't

know it was you till I looked up. Even then I wasn't sure. It was a kind of inspired guess, you might say—"

"Oh, get on with it!" snapped the bat. Kayak laughed.

"Yes sir!" he said, holding up his paw in a clumsy salute. "Anyway, like I said, I didn't know it was you, but I could tell there was a bat around when I seen all this dung that's lying around down here."

Redge laughed, and his weak little voice shuddered around the cave. The otter joined in, barking like a seal.

"Well, don't stand there like an idiot," said Redge, and he wiped his eyes with his wrinkled old fists. "Get out of the way."

"What for?"

"Well, if you stay where you are, I'll probably shit on your head at some stage. With a bit of luck."

The otter laughed uproariously at this, slapping his paw on the ground. He stopped when he ran out of breath, then moved a few paces to one side.

"Howling dogs, Redge!" he exclaimed. "That's done me, that has! I haven't had a laugh like that for ages."

"Nor me," said the bat.

The otter looked up at the clustered shadows around the top of the cave.

"How long's it been, Redge, since we last seen each other?"

"A long time," said Redge reflectively. "A very long time."

"Too true," said Kayak, nodding his head. His voice was quieter now, almost solemn. "We're not getting much younger, Redge."

The bat said nothing. And the otter did the same. They shared the silence as if it were something precious, letting it go on for a while. As usual it was the otter who broke it.

"Hey, Redge," he said, looking up around the ceiling of the cave, "is Number Two up there with you? Is she still asleep or something?"

"She's not here," said Redge.

"Oh, I see," said the otter, with a chuckle. "Gone and left you, has she? Flown off with someone else, eh?"

"No," said Redge in a small dark voice. "She's dead."

Kayak said nothing just for a moment. He stared at the ground.

"I'm sorry, Redge," he muttered. "I shouldn't have made a joke about it. You know what I'm like."

The bat nodded.

"Yes," he said quietly. "It's all right, Kayak. I understand."

Another silence. A different one.

"How did she die?" asked the otter. "Or don't you want to talk about it?"

Redge didn't want to, but he sighed and shrugged his shoulders.

"I found her," he intoned. "Last week. I came back from a hunting trip and she was—just dead. Lying on the ground under the alder trees. Lying there . . ."

He stopped and took a long breath.

"I was only away for a couple of hours. No longer than usual."

He stopped again. The otter thought he ought to say something.

"What was it, Redge—her heart, something like that?"

"No," said the bat. "Something attacked her. I don't know what. She was just lying there. What was left of her."

"Hell, Redge, I'm sorry . . ."

"Just one of her wings. And her head, staring at me.

The look on her face—she looked surprised, not terrified. I don't know . . ."

But he had to break off. The fur on his cheeks was damp with small tears and he wiped his nose with a finger.

Kayak looked unhappy too. He gazed at one of the cave walls and thought about what he should say next.

"Well, it's finished now," said Redge. "No point raking it all up again. Why don't you tell me what you're doing in this part of the world?"

"Oh, I always come down to the sea this time of year."

"I've never seen you here before."

"Well no, I usually go to that big bay down south."

"You mean the one past the headland?"

"That's right. It's not a bad little spot, all in all. I've been down there every summer for years now. Then I thought I'd like a change."

"And do you like it here?"

"Oh yes, Redge. Lovely place. There's more to eat, for a start. That's because it's where the old river meets the sea. You get freshwater and seawater fish all in the same spot. And shrimps and things. Lovely place. Don't know why I never came here before."

"Yes, I know," said the bat. "I always came here with Number Two. Every year. I didn't see any point in going anywhere else this time."

Kayak nodded and didn't speak.

"But tell me something," said Redge. "Isn't this your mating season?"

The otter laughed.

"No, that's all over now," he said. "That's why I'm here. I never come down to the coast till the new babies are out."

"Ah!" said the bat, his voice brightening. "How many this time?"

"Three," said Kayak happily. "Same as last year. Lovely they are, Redge. They're always lovely, of course. But this lot are the best ever. Mind you, I probably think that because they're the last I'm going to have."

"The last? Why's that?"

"Well, like I said, Redge, I'm getting on a bit now and—well, I'm not all that interested anymore."

The bat smiled broadly.

"I know what you mean," he said. "I gave all that up years ago."

"Quite right too," said Kayak decisively. "Waste of time as you get older. Anyway, this lot are definitely the last."

"Well, at least you're pleased with them."

"Oh yes," said the otter, with a glow in his voice. "They're bloody perfect. Two males, one little female. They're going to grow up lovely, I can tell."

"But don't you worry about leaving them so far away?"

"Oh, they're not far away at all. You know the second big bend in the river, past all them beech trees?"

"Yes," said the bat.

"Well, the nest is just there, at the beginning of the bend. In the bank behind the reed bed. It's just round the corner from here, really."

"That's good," said Redge. "I'd like to see them sometime. I think they might make me feel better."

"Oh, they would, Redge. No doubt about it. But what about your own family? You ought to go and stay with them for a while."

There was a wry sniff from the bat.

"To tell you the truth, Kayak, I don't know where any of them are. They're all grown up now, living their own lives somewhere. Anyway, we've always been a solitary breed, keeping ourselves to ourselves. I never needed any company. Except for Number Two."

He stopped and they both said nothing. The otter looked to the left and saw that the water level had risen. It was beginning to wash the floor of the cave, mingling with the rock pools.

"Tide's coming in fast, Redge," he announced. "It won't reach you up there, will it?"

"No," said the bat. "It comes up a long way, but there's always just enough room for me to stay dry."

Then his body went suddenly rigid. He hung perfectly still from the ceiling, listening as hard as he could.

"You know something, Redge, I think this—"

"Hush!" hissed the bat. "Shut up a minute. I can hear something moving outside."

"Pluck me, Redge!" breathed the otter. "I wish I had your ears, old mate. I bet you can hear a tree growing."

"Shut up, you idiot!"

The bat began to move across the ceiling, edging his way along to the point where it met one of the damp walls. As Kayak watched in silence, he made his way down to a small hole in the wall. It was just wide enough to fit his thin little body and he crawled through it. The otter raised an eyebrow. Redge reappeared.

"We've got a visitor," he said. There was a grin on his face.

"Ah good," said Kayak. "Three's a crowd, and there's nothing like a good crowd for having fun."

He trotted over to the mouth of the cave and looked out. It was early night outside. Away to the left, picking its way among the rocks strewn across the inlet, was an old dog-fox on its way down to the beach. The otter took one look at it and bolted back into the cave.

"Pissing fish, Redge!" he muttered, hiding against the far wall. "What the hell's that thing doing here?"

"Oh, he won't hurt you," said Redge, with a laugh. "That's only old Norris out looking for crabs."

"But it's a bloody fox, Redge!"

"So it is, Kayak. Norris the fox. And he's as docile as a rabbit. He's far too old to be anything else. Lost most of his teeth and he can hardly walk, let alone chase anything. That's why he spends his time down here, digging out a few baby crabs and eating seaweed."

"If he sees me, he might decide he needs to vary his diet!"

"If he sees you, he won't know what to do with you. He's too old, I tell you. Shall I call him in for a chat?"

"I'd rather you didn't," said Kayak hastily.

"Oh well, as you please." And the old bat shrugged. He stayed on the ledge just underneath the small gap in the wall, and they both watched from the shadows as Norris the fox walked past the cave with his nose in the water and his legs looking decidedly thin and very unsteady.

Only when the fox was long gone did Kayak the otter feel at all comfortable. Then he and the bat spent the best part of an hour in long conversation, punctuated by bursts of laughter and outbursts of singing. Neither of them could sing to save their lives, but that didn't stop them. When they were tired of singing they told jokes, each one longer and more crude than the last. Then they stopped for a rest.

"Hey, Redge, look at this!"

The bat looked.

"I can't see anything."

"Look, I'm floating!"

Redge nodded.

"You know, Kayak, you have the most amazing capacity for stating the obvious. First you inform me that my old friend Norris is a fox, and now you point out that you're floating."

"Well, I am."

"I can see that, you primitive. What's more, you've been floating for some time. The tide's been coming in."

"Now who's stating the obvious?" said the otter triumphantly.

"It seems to be the only form of statement you're equipped to cope with," retorted Redge, as pompously as he could. They both laughed.

"Well anyway," said Kayak, "how much further does it go up?"

"Not much more now," said the bat. "It comes up to this ledge, then a bit higher. That's all."

"Ah well, at least I'll be able to talk to you face-to-face instead of looking up all the time."

"I'm not sure I'm too happy with that," said Redge quietly.

"Why not?" frowned the otter.

"It means I'll have to look straight into your face, and that's something I wouldn't wish on my worst enemy."

They smiled. Redge looked away through the hole in the wall. "Well," he said, "it looks dark enough outside. I suppose you'll be off looking for food in a minute."

"Oh, there's no hurry," said the otter breezily.

"I wish this pain in my bones would go away," groaned the bat. "Then I could go out looking for food myself."

"Can't you fly at all?"

"No, can't even get off the ground. I can still crawl a bit, of course. I'll go out later on and see if I can pouch a beetle or something up on top of the cliff. In fact . . ." He looked out through the hole again. "I think I might go up there now."

"Oh, I wouldn't do that, Redge."

"I'll be all right, don't worry. I've done it before."

"I still don't think it's a good idea," said Kayak.

"Well, why not?"

The otter shrugged.

"I just don't think there's any point."

"Of course there is, you idiot. I could do with a quick meal, and if I go up there I'll get one."

"That's not quite what I meant," began the otter.

"Well, what exactly did you mean?"

Kayak looked up sharply. His eyes were suddenly very narrow and his voice was different.

"Just this, Redge. There's no point your going up on the cliff because you don't need to eat anything. I'm going to make sure you never need food again."

The bat opened his mouth then quickly closed it. There was silence again for a moment and he could hear his heart racing away in his chest.

"I don't understand you, Kayak," he said slowly. "At least, I hope I don't."

"Ah, but you do, Redge. You know just what I'm talking about."

"But it's not possible," said the bat. "Not me. You can't really want to—"

"What makes you think I can't?"

"Well, I just know it, Kayak. We've been friends for such a long—anyway, you don't eat bats."

"Don't be so bloody simple, Redge," scowled the otter. "I eat mice, don't I? And rats and voles. It's all the same thing."

Redge felt inclined to tell him that it wasn't the same thing at all, but this didn't seem the time or place.

"But not me, Kayak," he said lamely. "You can't really want to eat someone you know so well."

The otter looked at him with absolutely nothing in his eyes.

"Who do you think ate Number Two?" he said gravely.

The bat's jaw fell open. He inched away along the small ledge, his eyes nearly heaving out of his head. He didn't say anything—but then he didn't have to. The look on his face was enough.

"Yes, Redge, I know." Kayak's voice was flat and mirthless. There was a hint of regret in it. "I'm not proud of it, but there it is. She died like a lady, Redge, if that's any consolation. Didn't even cry out. She wanted to save you, keep you right out of it."

The bat shook his head.

"You killed Number Two," was all he could say.

"Don't make it any harder than it is, Redge."

"Why her?" snapped the bat, his eyes glinting fierce in the darkness. "Why kill Number Two? She couldn't hurt you."

The otter paddled his feet in the rising water and gave his tail a guilty little twitch.

"Food, Redge. That's all there was to it. You know what a hard winter it's been. I needed food for my female while she was having the little ones."

"You killed Number Two for food?" There was nothing in the bat's voice. A trace of disbelief perhaps, no more.

"I haven't come here to justify myself, Redge," growled Kayak. "I've come here to eat you."

Redge looked him in the eye.

"What makes you think I'll let you?" he said.

The otter smiled.

"You can't stop me, Redge. You know that. You can't fly and you can't run away. And you're not going to try and fight your way out . . ."

Redge looked at him. The situation certainly seemed cut and dried. On one hand, a large healthy male otter, hungry and calmly determined, almost filling the little cave with his body. On the other, a wrinkled bat half the size of the otter's head, his bones full of old age and rheumatism. No contest.

Redge saw the water creeping upwards. He knew the otter had only to wait a little longer before he could reach out and crunch the bat's shrivelled body in his teeth. Neither of them spoke. The old bat glanced around the cave, then drew back his head, jerked it forward, and spat in Kayak's face.

The otter let loose a short stream of oaths, groping at the spittle in his eye. He thrust his paw up along the wall of the cave, but found nothing. He ducked his head in the water to clear his eye, then looked up. Redge was gone. Escaped through the crack in the wall. Kayak cursed again, but only briefly. Then he turned and dived under the surface. In no time at all he'd reached the bottom of the drowned cave and found the way out. From there he made his way straight back up to the surface.

He was outside the cave now, looking up out of the water at the side of the limestone cliff. There was no moon, but it was brighter than inside the cave, and he had no trouble spotting the tiny figure of Redge the bat crawling slowly up the cliff. He smiled, acknowledging the stubborn ingenuity of his old friend. Then he swam over to the cliff wall and found what he was looking for. A path leading to the top.

It was steep and very narrow but better than nothing, and Kayak scrambled up it without delay. He didn't like climbing and he wasn't very good at it, but that made no great difference. Before long he had struggled his way up to the flat summit of the cliff.

Here there was nothing but cropped grass and a high wind that smelt of seaweed and dead crabs. He had the forest to his right and the far edge of the cliff to his left, overlooking the sea. Almost on the edge itself was the single lonely figure of the old bat, with the dark grey sky reaching down to the blackish sea in the background. Kayak walked across the grass towards him.

"I've got to hand it to you, Redge," he shouted, his mouth full of salt wind. "You never give up, do you?"

He came right up close to the bat, only a couple of paces away.

"But it's all over now, old mate," he said quietly.

Redge looked back at him and didn't speak.

"It's finished, Redge. There's nowhere left to run."

"You killed Number Two," snarled the bat. "I can't forgive you for that."

The otter had had enough. He lunged at the bat with his mouth open and his eyes half-closed. He hit the grass with his body, and his mouth snapped shut. But Redge wasn't there.

Kayak scowled and scratched at the grass near his feet. Then he realised what had happened and crouched his way to the extreme edge of the cliff. He looked down. The rocks at the bottom seemed miles away. He saw the waves blasting foam all over them. But no Redge.

He looked quickly to the left, then to the right. He turned slowly round till his back was to the sea. And still he couldn't see anyone. Just then, there was a soft puckering of wings—and the old bat fluttered down to earth a few yards in front of him.

Kayak couldn't believe his eyes. He pointed at Redge with his paw.

"You can fly," he said hoarsely.

"As always, my dear Kayak," said the bat acidly, "your aptitude for stating the self-evident remains unchallenged."

The otter tried to speak but he had nothing to say. He just stood there with his mouth open.

"Yes, I was lying," said Redge. "Simple as that. And why? Because I knew. All the time I knew what you'd done."

"How?"

"I saw you kill Number Two," said the bat calmly. The otter hung his head. "I was on my way home—but I was just too late. She was already in pieces when I reached her. I saw an otter skulking away in the night, and I knew she would never have come down to speak to an otter unless she knew who it was." He paused. "You're the only otter we know. So I knew from the start that it was you, but there was nothing I could do about it." He paused again and the wind filled the silence. "Nothing, that is, until now."

The otter raised his head.

"Now?" he echoed. "What do you mean by that? There's nothing you can do now."

"Nothing?" said Redge, smiling only with his mouth.

"No, nothing. All right, so you've made me look a fool,

but that's all you can do. Go away, Redge. Go away somewhere and forget about it."

The bat sucked in his cheeks.

"I intend to do just that," he said. "But first I'm going somewhere else."

Kayak wasn't interested.

"Where?" he said blankly.

"Oh, just north to the river," said Redge flippantly. "To the second bend, where the reeds grow in a large bed. To a nest in the bank—"

"No!" roared the otter, staggering forward.

"No?" said the bat placidly. "Can't I go and visit your little ones? Oh, what a pity!"

"You won't touch them," growled Kayak. "So help me, Redge, if you go anywhere near them, I'll break your back—"

"You'll do nothing!" cried the bat. "You can't get back to them in time to stop me. And you'll never find me after I've finished with them!"

The otter gave an anguished cry and leapt forward, reaching out, straining to catch him. But Redge simply lifted himself off the ground and fluttered round in a circle, flapping his wings and avoiding each of Kayak's desperate leaps with ease.

"I'm only going to visit the little darlings," he laughed. "Their mother will soon go out hunting and leave them to sleep. And to me!"

"No, Redge! Not the little ones. They're all I've got left."

"I know how you feel," nodded the bat. "Number Two was all I had left."

"But they're only babies, Redge. They never done you any harm."

"How often did Number Two do you any harm?"

"Redge, please." The otter was crying now. The tears choked his mouth. "I can't live without them. For pity's sake, Redge—"

"Tell me about the pity you showed Number Two."

"Sod it, Redge!" screamed the otter. "She's dead. Killing my babies won't bring her back."

Redge flew off and landed on the grass some distance away. This time Kayak knew it was no use chasing after him.

"You're right," cried the bat. "Nothing can bring her back. But I won't leave her killer to spend his last years in peace with his family. You took my Number Two from me, Kayak. I'll take your babies from you. A tooth for a tooth!"

"You don't mean it, Redge," sobbed the otter. "I know you. You won't hurt them."

"I'll pluck their tongues out!" yelled the bat. "They're probably still blind and hairless, the poor little dabs. All safe and snug in their nest of reeds. I'll tear their throats away! I'll suck the blood out of them!"

"No!" squealed Kayak. He rolled on the windswept grass with his paws over his ears, and tears soaking his face. When he finally stopped and looked up, he caught a last glimpse of the old bat flying away towards the forest, going north.

"No, Redge," he murmured to himself. "Not the little ones. Redge, not the babies." Then he stood quite still, threw back his head, and poured a long agonised roar into the night. The wind blew it away.

The otter's eyes were hot and full of tears as he turned and trudged to the edge of the cliff. He looked down at the restless surf and the same crashing rocks. It was all blurred now, indistinct. Nothing but a haze of grey and black, and the continual noise of the waves. The wind and the smell of seaweed.

"Redge." The otter was quite incoherent by now. "Babies, Redge. Best ever. Can't bring her back. Not living without them."

He stood up on his hind legs, just for a second—then keeled over to one side. He fell through the air on his back, hit the waiting rocks at the foot of the cliff, and split open like a sack of blood. The sea washed him away.

A quick moist fluttering of membrane wings and Redge the bat landed on the top edge of the cliff. He looked down and watched the waves washing Kayak's body out to sea. The wind blustered through his fur and whiskers, but Redge didn't feel it. He was busy weeping. His best friend was dead.

It was over now. Really and completely finished. For days and nights on end he'd waited and longed for this moment. A tooth for a tooth. With Number Two dead, he'd been left with nothing else to live for. And now here he was, alone in the moment itself. He looked up at the bleak horizon, then down again. What was it, he wondered, this vengeance he'd been yearning for, this final reckoning? The smattered body of an otter, and nothing. Revenge and rough justice—but Redge was still alone. He knew the otter had been right. Nothing could bring her back.

There was no more thinking to be done, nothing left to cry about, so he waved his ugly little wings and flew off into the night. But he flew south, away from the second bend in the river, not towards it.

FANULLA

IN SUMMER, EACH OF THE PLOUGHED fields next to the forest is piled high with a mixture of wheat and corn. Hidden and stifled by it. And in amongst the wheat and corn there are nests. Built by harvest mice, inhabited by harvest mice. Most of them.

The largest of these nests is near the very centre of the widest wheatfield, high above the ground. A solid woven ball of grass and plaited cornleaves, supported by thick white stalks.

Outside, the sun is hot. Inside, on a bed of green hay, a dormouse is sleeping. Soft, plump, deeply asleep. Warm and very still, with a white tip on her tail and no smile on her face. Fat Fanulla's snoring.

Fanulla. Fa-nool-la. A strange enough name for a dormouse. The field was never her natural home. The nest isn't her own. She stole it. Now, as the air feels the heat, no-one disturbs her. Fat Fanulla's dreaming.

Nothing moves in the nest. No-one speaks. No breeze, no whispers in the corn. Just fat Fanulla's breathing.

Soon she'll wake up and think about what happened last week.

It was the hottest day of the year. The clouds had all been burned to death and every ditch and stream was half-filled with lukewarm water. No-one could sleep in a heat like this, not even the soft plump dormouse. She got up to stretch her legs.

Her nose appeared through the tight grass wall of the nest. Then her head and half her body. Everything was too bright out here. She had to keep her eyes tightly shut for a while. The sun was far too hot but in a way she enjoyed it. It was another day, another batch of hours in a foreign place—and she was still alive. It was something to be pleased about, despite the heat.

She had her eyes shut and her nose quivering in the air when she heard a loud rustle in the corn down to her right. Her eyes opened at once and she slipped back into the nest, leaving only her face exposed.

The rustling noise grew louder. The stalks of wheat parted and something slid out between them. It stopped, and Fanulla couldn't see what it was. She didn't dare come out to investigate, so she waited for the creature to move again. And it didn't.

Eventually she couldn't stand it any longer. Her head inched out of the nest and she looked down. She couldn't see the creature at first, but when she turned her head round to the side she caught sight of it. And her face started to fidget. It was a snake.

An adder. Dark grey, with green-black markings down both sides, lying very still. It turned its head and looked up. When it saw the dormouse it did nothing except gaze at her with its copper-coloured eyes. She stared at it and didn't move. Then she spoke to it.

"What do you want?" she said tersely.

The adder looked at her as if the answer were obvious.

"I want to get out of here," it said, in a dry flaking voice.

Fanulla shrugged her shoulders.

"Well, you can't," she said.

The adder licked its face.

"Why not?" it said sulkily. "We've been here long enough."

"No," said Fanulla. "I like it here."

"It's all right for you. You've got a cool nest and plenty to eat. But I need the open spaces. The rocks and sand-hills. I feel closed-in here. I can't move easily."

The dormouse pouted.

"Well," she said easily, "can I help it if you're a crip-ple?"

The snake hissed, spittling out its anger. But it was true. The whole of its left side was paralysed.

"Go on then," it lisped. "Mock me as usual. But where would you be without me?"

She laughed.

"And where would you be without the food I bring you? You know you can't catch anything for yourself. You'd be finished without me and you know it. You'd starve to death."

"No!" said the snake.

"No?" she smiled. "Well, if you're so sure, leave me. I'll stay here and you can go off to your sand-hills alone."

The snake muttered something unintelligible. There was foam on its mouth.

"Go on," she said. "Leave if you want to. You can do it."

"Yes!" spat the adder. "I can survive without the likes of you. I've done it before."

She laughed again, longer and deliberately louder.

"Oh yes," she chuckled. "You survived. And how well you did it! Remember how I found you? Remember?"

The snake hissed and looked away.

"The state you were in!" she went on. "Thin as a nettle and nearly dead with thirst. And how long will you last this time, on your own, out in the open? What about the hawks, and the weasels? What about the crows? What happens when they find out the mighty Rasp is no more than a slithering wreck? An invalid, a worm—"

She was interrupted by a sudden wild hiss from the viper as it whirled round to face her, reaching out with its tongue. It was too far away to harm her but she couldn't help recoiling. The expression on the snake's face was pure venom.

"One day," it said slowly. "One day you'll change your tune."

The dormouse sighed. She'd heard it all before.

"Why don't you go away?" she said wearily. "The very sight of you makes me sick."

The viper snarled and its body shivered on the ground. It glared up at the smug little dormouse and twisted its tongue.

"I hate you," it breathed. "I wish I could kill you."

Fanulla shrugged.

"I know," she said breezily. "It must be very irritating for you. Still, look on the bright side. Things could be worse. You might have been crippled down both sides!"

The snake growled and turned away. It couldn't bear to see the smile on her face.

"Now go," she said. "I've got better things to do than listen to you whining."

"But I hate this place!" moaned the adder, hitting the ground with its tail. "We've got to go somewhere else."

"No," she said. "We'll stay here till I think it's time to leave."

The adder rolled its body around in the dust, twitching with frustration and biting the dirt in its fury. Fanulla watched it impassively and waited for the convulsions to die down. She looked at the long crumpled body and the deformed V-shape on its forehead. And thought nothing. The viper looked up.

"Food," it said, the voice brittle as a dead leaf. "I haven't eaten for three days."

"That's because I haven't fed you for three days," she said dryly.

"I know that!" it snapped. "I've got to eat again, soon."

"Yes," she said. "Soon."

"When?"

"When I can be bothered."

The snake looked away, resigned to the situation. It made no show of anger.

"I'm not asking for the earth," it muttered. "Just a bite to eat."

"I know, I know," she said impatiently. The sun was hurting her face.

"Then feed me."

"I will."

"When?"

"Tonight, if I can. Now go away and leave me alone."

But Rasp was already on his way, dragging slowly and painfully along between the stalks of wheat and out of sight. The dormouse didn't watch him go. She went back into the nest to get out of the sun.

Things had changed for fat Fanulla. She'd been a princess once, plump and beautiful, in a distant hedgerow. But there were enemies to be made there. Dormice with jealous hearts and soft murmuring voices, whispering in the ear of the chief dormouse. And he'd believed them, her strong regal lover. Believed everything they told him and pushed her out of the hedgerow, out into the ditch, away from her royal nest and her new-born babies.

The world outside had no great respect for reputation and rank. It was a world of huge death. Claws and hooked beaks and screaming. A world in which a dormouse, even a dormouse princess, was a very small thing.

And then she'd met the snake. The crippled adder, starving quietly to death in a bed of nettles. She'd made a pact with him. She would bring him food and he would stay close to her, protect her with his slivering tongue and his show of strength.

He'd hated her from the start, of course. Hated the way she laughed and looked down on him, hated his dependence on her.

On the other hand, she felt nothing for him. She never thought of him unless he was there. The sound of his dry gravelled voice irritated her and she despised his weakness. But not very much. She preferred to sleep.

The nest was a good place for sleep. A pair of fastidious harvest mice had lived in it with their litter of well-groomed infants. But they were all gone now. The snake had seen to that. And now it was her nest.

Before long she would have to move out, she knew. The snake was impatient to leave and she couldn't keep him in the wheatfield for ever. And that was a shame. It suited her very well. The nest was comfortable and the field itself a stronghold, a maze of escape routes. Besides, there was plenty of food to be found in it. For herself, and for the snake . . .

The sun rolled into late afternoon, baking the cornfield on its way. Nothing moved and there was hardly a sound. Everything and everyone was flattened by the heat, hiding from it, asleep or itching for sleep; in nests, under leaves or scattered grass. There was no disturbance, no interference from outside, nothing to infiltrate the quiet white field. It was in a world of its own.

And fat Fanulla was half-asleep. She woke up and scratched her breast and belly. There was nothing to do, as usual. She went to the half-open door of the nest and looked out, yawned and smacked her lips, rubbed the drowsiness from her eyes.

Not far away, something was moving. Fanulla saw it right away. Something tussling along the top of the corn, jumping from stalk to stalk. She squinted through the glare of the sun and saw it was a mouse. Just a mouse, she thought—but better than nothing. She disappeared back into the nest and watched it carefully.

It was too big to be a harvest mouse. Or any kind of real mouse. It was golden brown, broad-shouldered, young and male. A dormouse with a white-tipped tail. Fanulla looked at it questioningly. It was the only other dormouse she'd ever seen in the wheatfield.

He seemed totally unconcerned about the heat. He was bounding along quite merrily, swinging from one wheatstalk to the next and whistling through his teeth. He passed Fanulla's nest without so much as a glance, but then he caught sight of her as she edged her way out into the open—and he stopped whistling. He looked her slowly up and down, staring at her as if he'd never seen another dormouse before.

"What's the matter?" she said in a cherry-ripe voice. "Haven't you ever seen another dormouse before?"

The mouse licked his mouth.

"Well yes," he began. Then he stopped. She laughed. A laugh that Rasp the adder had never heard her use.

"It's all right, strongman," she cooed, "I won't hurt you."

He looked at her and wiped his mouth with a paw.

"You're very beautiful," he said. Fanulla smiled.

"Well," she nodded, "forthright as well as handsome. That's quite a combination."

"Why are you so beautiful?" He made it sound a perfectly ordinary question.

"Why?" she said coyly. "Well, I'm not so sure that I am . . ."

"Yes you are. You're the most beautiful female I've ever known."

She raised her eyebrows as she smiled.

"Oh? And how many have you known?"

He lifted his head just a little defiantly.

She laughed.

"Of course," she said. "More than enough, no doubt. What's your name?"

"I haven't got one," he said quickly. Too quickly.

"You must have. Everyone has a name."

"Not me."

"Why not?"

He shrugged.

"How should I know? I've never had one, that's all."

She gave him a light quizzical look.

"Is it a name you're ashamed of?"

"No, it's not! It's a perfectly good name—"

He stopped. She smiled again.

"Tell me what it is," she coaxed. "I won't laugh."

He shook his head.

"But you must tell me," she insisted. "What am I supposed to call you? And anyway you shouldn't be afraid to tell me, a good-looking young heavyweight like you."

He looked down at his feet and swayed on the top of his stalk of wheat, hanging on with all four legs.

"I'm not afraid to tell you," he muttered.

"Then tell me."

"But it's such a stupid name," he groaned. "I hate it."

"Well, just tell me and we'll forget about it."

He sighed.

"It's Pickle," he said, very quickly and not very loudly. She suppressed a grin.

"That's not so bad," she said.

"Yes it is," he said gloomily. "It's appalling. It makes me feel so small. Like a baby."

Her eyes narrowed.

"You don't look like a baby, you know that . . ."

He looked up and saw her half-smiling at him. There was something about her that quickened his pulse.

"No," he said idiotically, not knowing what else to say.

"Where are you going?" she changed the subject.

He pointed with his paw.

"Over there, to the forest to see my female."

"Ah," she said slowly. "Your female. What's her name?"

"Pipette," he said, with something like pride in his voice. "I've got to be there by sunset, so I'm travelling by day."

She nodded.

"Pipette," she said. "That's a pretty little name. Is she pretty too?"

"Well," he said pensively, "she's not nearly as beautiful as you. But I like her."

"Yes," she said quietly, "I'm sure you do."

A pause. He ended it with a small cough.

"Are you going to tell me your name?" he asked.

"Fanulla." She said it without hurrying. Pickle was impressed.

"Fanulla," he said. "Fa-noola. Now that really is a lovely name."

She smiled.

"Is that your nest?" he asked. "Have you always lived there?"

"No," she said, answering both questions at once. "And I shall go away soon."

"Oh!" he said. "I shall miss you."

She laughed quietly.

"Well," she said, "you really are forthright, aren't you? But you won't really miss me. You don't know me well enough."

"I know," he said. "I know that, but . . . well, I shall miss you all the same."

She wiped the first touch of sweat from her nose.

"Yes," she said, "but it's not worth it. I'm old enough to be your mother."

"No you're not!"

"Oh yes. I'm older than I look."

He looked.

"Well, I don't care. I think—"

"I know," she said. "You think I'm beautiful. And so I am. So are you. But you have a female to go to, remember?"

"Yes," he said. "I haven't forgotten."

"You'd better go to her now," she added. "Otherwise you won't be there by sunset."

He nodded, said nothing, and looked away towards the forest. In the silence they both felt the sticking weight of the sun.

"Would you rather stay here for a while?" Her voice made no promises. She used nothing but the words to invite him. And he hesitated.

"I want to," he said, without looking at her. "You know I want to. But I don't think I can."

"You can," she said, and her voice was coy again, "if you really want to."

He looked at her, but his mind was only half made up. She shrugged and turned away, slowly, languidly.

"Well, I'm going back inside," she said. "It's too hot out here."

And she was gone, leaving him to stare at the nest and nibble the insides of his cheeks. He looked away again, across the teeming cornfield to the edge of the forest. It was very far away. The muscles in his face ached from squinting in the sun.

"You're right," he said with a weak smile, as he pushed through the half-closed door of the nest, "it's too hot outside."

Fanulla said nothing, but her smile was welcome enough. She stretched herself out along the grassy bed. A long slow-moving stretch, all fur and faint sighing. Pickle didn't move until she looked up at him.

"Come along, strongman," she said wickedly. "I won't melt in your mouth . . ."

The rest of the afternoon passed slowly and luxuriously for the big young mouse as he explored Fanulla's short sumptuous body. And when evening arrived he was lying with his nose against the back of her neck and a limp little smile on his mouth. There was no expression in Fanulla's face.

"It's time for you to go," she said lazily.

"Yes," he agreed, and pushed his nose further into her neck.

"I mean it," she said.

He made a noise deep in his throat and bit her shoulder.

"Fool," she said, with a short laugh. He laughed too.

"I don't want to go," he murmured.

"You have to. Your little female will be waiting."

"I don't care."

She smiled.

"But will she go on waiting?"

"I don't know."

She turned round to nestle her face in his chest, but he rolled over and put his cheek on her belly. And she let him lie there, pulling his ear with her paw. He was so big and powerful, so very young. She could almost have felt maternal towards him. Almost.

"Well, if you're not going to see her, you'll have to go home."

"I want to stay here."

"Yes, I know. But you can't stay here for ever."

"Why not?"

She slapped his shoulder as she laughed.

"It's time to go home, strongman. And no more arguments."

He lifted his head and rolled off her belly.

"Oh, all right," he grouched. "But I'll be back."

"Will you now?"

"Yes I will. Tomorrow. And the next day. And the next—"

"And what makes you so sure I want you to come back?"

He looked at her. There was a dry smile on her face and her eyebrows were raised.

"Oh, but you do!" he said. "I mean . . . well, you do, don't you?"

She laughed at the imploring tone in his voice and fiddled with his scanty whiskers.

"Well now, strongman, perhaps I do. But now you must go home."

"Yes," he said, and he put his head back on her belly. "I suppose you're right. I'd better leave soon. It's a long way to go."

"How far?"

"Around the edge of the forest, to the east. There's a large hedgerow across the ditch."

"A hedgerow?" she said softly. He didn't notice the tone of her voice.

"Yes," he said. "It's full of dormice. My whole family lives there. You ought to come and visit us sometime. You might even want to live there yourself."

A hedgerow, she was thinking. It could only be *her* hedgerow. She'd been a princess there.

"No," she said quietly. "I'll stay here."

"I don't blame you," he nodded. "I like it here too." He

kissed her hip. She said nothing and didn't move. Pickle lifted his head again.

"Did you hear that?"

"What?" she said.

"There was a noise. Outside."

"No," she said, but he got up and went to the door of the nest. He listened hard.

"There!" he whispered. "The same noise. Something's out there."

She got up too and moved over to the door.

"Can you tell what it is?" she asked. He shook his head.

"I'm going to have a look."

She didn't say anything as he pushed his head out of the nest. It was still very bright outside, but there was no great heat, no glare from the sun. A few shadows from the forest, a thin breeze. And, wrapped around a nearby wheatstalk, the mottled body of a grey snake.

Pickle's head disappeared back into the nest very quickly.

"What is it?" said Fanulla.

He shook his head.

"We've got to get out of here," he breathed.

"Why?" she frowned. "Let me have a look."

"No!" He put his body between hers and the doorway. "There's something out there."

"Well, what is it?" she asked, but he wouldn't tell her.

"It doesn't matter," he said. "Just an animal. But it might be dangerous, so we'd better get out. If it decides to come up here we'll be trapped."

"What do you want to do?" she asked.

He bit his lower lip and thought for a moment.

"Well, we'll have to move out very quietly. When we're

out of range we can start running and it'll never catch us."

She nodded slowly.

"All right," she said. "If you're sure we can do it."

"I'm not sure at all," he said curtly. "But it's all we can do. I'll go first. Follow me out onto the stalk that's holding this nest up, and we'll take it from there."

"Which stalk? There are three of them."

"The biggest one, on the right."

She nodded and he shouldered his way out of the nest.

They moved very slowly, inching out of the doorway onto the green-white cornstalk and staying very close together. Fanulla looked down and saw the motionless figure of the snake.

He was early, as expected. She scowled at him, but the snake wasn't looking at her. Pickle reached behind him and touched her shoulder. He pointed to a thick outgrowing leaf just above their heads. A leaf that reached right across to the next patch of wheat. It was clear that if they managed to get across to that patch they could soon lose themselves in the dense tangle of corn on the right.

Pickle went first, clambering slowly upwards, his body hidden behind the wheatstalk. There was no way the viper could see him as he climbed. Fanulla followed close behind, peeping round the side of the stalk to see what the snake was doing. He looked fast asleep.

Pickle reached the point where the leaf joined the stalk, and turned to check that Fanulla was all right behind him. Then he started to creep out along the leaf itself.

Right on cue, the adder made its move. It uncoiled itself from around its own stalk, crabbed its way across the dust, and stopped directly underneath the wheatleaf.

Pickle glanced down at the snake and found he couldn't look away from it. He stared at the permanent scowl on its brow and its dangling tongue. Its eyes were the colour of dried blood. He shuddered.

"Come on!" he gasped—and turned to help Fanulla across the creaking leaf. But she was already there, standing very close. There was no fear or urgency in her face.

"Quick!" he said. "Run when I do and we can still make it."

"No," she said flatly.

His eyes were wide now.

"It's all right!" he hissed. "It can't catch us once we're across."

Fanulla shook her head.

"We can't both make it," she said.

"Of course we can."

"We won't."

"What are you talking about? Come on—before it's too late!"

He grabbed her foreleg but she pulled away from him.

"Goodbye, strongman," she said. And punched him in the face with her paw.

He fell backwards more through surprise than the force of the blow. She had time to catch the last look on his face before he dropped off the edge of the curling leaf.

He hit the ground like a lump of mud and all the breath was kicked out of him. Even so, his brain screamed at him to move away—and he did, scrabbling at the dirt with his hindlegs and rolling over on his side. But the snake was too fast for him. It was too crippled to chase anything, but it could still strike from close range—and it lunged, trapped the wriggling dormouse in its jaws, and paralysed him with the force of its bite. Then it began to swallow him all in one piece.

Fanulla watched all this with a calm face, without feeling anything. Except, perhaps, a prickle of satisfaction. The big young mouse had come from the hedgerow. And the hedgerow had turned her into an exile. Now, in a small way, she'd struck back. While the adder gulped his first meal for three days, she turned and went back to her nest.

And the night came, black and refreshing. Fanulla woke up from a last fretting slumber and left the nest in search of food. First she sniffed the air outside and had a good look round. She was by habit a nocturnal creature, so she could see perfectly well in the darkness. She saw only the wheat and the dry splitting earth. And a small crouching shape lurking behind the nearest wheatstalk, perched on a thin stem. Fanulla peered at it. She moved slowly away from the nest, up along a corn cob. She looked again and saw it was a dormouse.

Another one, she thought. The place is crawling with them today. The dormouse wasn't looking at her. It was just squatting there doing nothing, wrapped up in its own thoughts.

"Who are you?" said Fanulla in a clear voice. The newcomer was startled by the sound but showed no real fear.

"Please," it said in a tiny female voice, "I won't be long. Just let me stay a little longer and I'll go away."

"Stay as long as you like," said Fanulla. "I don't own this place. I only want to know who you are."

There was no reply.

"Well, what's your name?" said Fanulla in a sterner voice. Then she heard the little dormouse sobbing and she frowned.

"Why are you crying?" she asked, without caring one way or the other. The dormouse lifted her head out from her hands.

"He's dead," she said softly, and her lips couldn't keep still.

"Who is?" said Fanulla.

"My friend. We hadn't known each other very long. He was going to be my lover."

Fanulla shrugged.

"I'm very sorry," she said, in a tone that meant almost the opposite.

"No you're not," said the other, shaking her head. "You can't be. You killed him."

Fanulla raised an eyebrow and smiled.

"So," she said, "you're Pipette."

"Yes."

"How did you know he was dead?"

Pipette looked away across the top of the cornfield.

"I have friends here. They saw you. You pushed him down and the snake did the rest."

Fanulla said nothing.

"I was too far away," said the little dormouse. "There was nothing I could do to help." She sniffed once or twice but there were no tears this time. "Anyway," she went on,"I just wanted to see where he died, to think about him one last time. And to see you."

Fanulla didn't like the sound of that.

"Why?" she said.

"I wanted to see who you were, what you were like. When he didn't come to me at sunset I knew he wouldn't have stopped for any ordinary female. You're very beautiful."

Fanulla said nothing again. She looked away, at nothing in particular.

"I'm not beautiful," said Pipette. "So it wasn't hard for you to make an impression on him."

She started to cry again, very softly.

"Don't do that," said Fanulla, with a certain tenderness. "You'll find someone else sooner or later."

"Oh, I'm not crying because of that," said Pipette. She sniffed again and wiped one of her eyes with the back of her paw. "I'm not crying for myself at all. I'm crying for him."

"That won't help him now."

Pipette cleared her throat. Her eyes were nearly dry again.

"No," she agreed. "You're right. I'm not doing anyone much good staying here."

She climbed down the wheatstalk. When she was on the ground she looked up.

"I'm right to be unhappy," she said. "He was worth a tear or two, wasn't he?"

"Yes," said Fanulla. And she meant it. "He was worth more than that."

"Perhaps," said Pipette, with a sad little shrug. "But then you knew him better than I ever did."

"What do you mean?" said Fanulla, with a short yawn.

"Well," said the little dormouse—and her eyes were like stone—"you were his mother."

Fanulla's mouth was open but she couldn't speak. She looked down at the ground but there was nobody there. She turned away and stared into space.

It didn't take her long to realise the dormouse had told her the truth. She remembered the white tip on Pickle's tail, the fact that he came from the same hedgerow, the way she'd felt about him. Her son. He'd been skin-close to her. She'd felt and smelt him and never known, never even guessed. She recalled the look on his face as he fell off the leaf towards the snake.

She looked up at the black sky and laughed, loud and bitterly. Then, abruptly, she stopped and did nothing but look faintly miserable. Before long she climbed down the cornstalk and scampered away through the field.

"Where do you think you're going?" said a dull grey voice. She looked and saw the viper just ahead of her. He was lying quite placidly in a clump of white weeds, nursing his tail in his coils.

"You killed my son," she said.

"What are you drivelling about?"

"Your afternoon snack. It was my son."

The snake shut its mouth.

"I'm going away," she went on. "I may be back in a week."

"Well can't you wait a bit?" grumbled the snake. "I haven't finished digesting—I mean, I'm not ready yet."

She looked at him and quickly looked away.

"You're not coming with me." It wasn't an order, just a statement of fact. The snake's face twitched.

"I'll die if you leave me. You know that."

"Yes," she shrugged. "I know that."

"And so will you."

"Sometime, yes."

"But you can't live without me." The adder's voice was urgent now. His tongue was fluttering. "You won't be able to protect yourself. You have to let me come with you."

"No," she said, looking him square in the face. "I don't have to do anything."

She turned and walked away. The adder snarled and made a desperate lunge at her, but he knew she was too far away. As she ran away into the forest of wheatstalks, he felt a seizure in his left flank and rolled over hissing with pain. Nobody heard him.

The days went past. Five or six of them in a row. And Fanulla was still alive. She moved through the first bleak rays of another morning and stood at the crest of a small rise, a steep ragged slope of sand. At the bottom there was a familiar bed of nettles, sprayed with pebbles and broken slate. And the long body of a dead snake, stripped of its skin. Surrounded by a reeling crowd of wasps and horseflies, drunk with blood. The dormouse stayed and watched for a while, then hurried back to the nest in the cornfield. Back to sleep.

And now she's awake. Fat Fanulla's up and stretching her limbs, smacking her lips. Smiling again. She thinks back to that long night of death, but it was a week ago and she's nearly forgotten it. And her son? Well, she never asked him to be her son, did she? She has no time for black thoughts. There are things to do, another day to get through, a soft lashing sound somewhere away in the distance. She yawns and wipes her eyes open.

It's hot in the nest, afternoon hot. Time for a walk, something to drink. The lashing sound is louder and she hears it, goes out of the nest to meet it. There's nothing there, but the sound stays and grows. She looks around and feels curiously disinterested as the noise fills the air, stamping out all other sounds. And she doesn't see the bright red combine harvester as it carves through the corn, grinding and churning the stalks and stems and flaccid ears of wheat, slicing through a hundred woven nests before splashing heedlessly on to the far end of the dry white field.

The silence comes back, very slowly. And there's no-one around to see what's been going on, to look down and call out for everyone to hear. No-one knows and no-one wants to know . . .

Fat Fanulla's dead.

U G

ONE OF THE FOREST LEGENDS LIVED in amongst a clump of trees somewhere in the west, where the ground was nearly always wet and smudged with mud. It was almost a clearing but not quite.

Standing all alone in this small opening was a fat clean robin with a polished beak. It was glancing around and muttering impatiently to itself, lifting a leg from time to time and cleaning the mud off it. It was plainly looking for someone.

It hopped from one slumping bank of ferns to the next, from tree to tree, looking up down and around, with no luck. It grew more and more exasperated, but it didn't stop looking. And then it came to the hump of a root rising up out of the mud near a tree, forming a kind of grotto. The robin looked inside. And got the shock of its life.

There was an eye under the root. A big bulbous eye, red and wet as a gumboil. And attached behind this eye was the gnarled brown body of the biggest bull toad the robin had ever seen.

The quick bird nipped back out of reach and stared at the toad without being able to speak. The toad's only movement came from his throat muscles pumping regular lumps of air down his windpipe.

"What do you bloody want?" he growled, in a deep pit of a voice. He was in a fearfully bad temper that morning. His shoulder had started aching again. The robin cleared its throat.

"I have a message for you," it piped. "From the Great Lord. From Arcan himself."

The toad snorted.

"Oh, I see," he scoffed. "Calls himself the Great Lord now, does he? Well, what does the pompous old idiot want now?"

It had obviously never occurred to the robin to think of the great Arcan as either pompous or idiotic—and it was quite taken aback. But one look was enough to convince it that the big toad was not the sort of animal to split hairs with.

"He wishes to see you," it said, with its beak in the air.

"Is that all?"

"That is his message."

"What exactly does he want?"

"No doubt he will inform you when he sees you."

"Tell him to bugger off."

The robin was now really quite shocked. It hadn't expected a reception like this.

"But it really is very important that you go and see him."

"Cobblers."

"It is most urgent."

"Tell him to go sit on a carrot. I'm busy."

The robin wriggled on the spot as if it had an itch in its rump. The toad didn't notice. He'd turned away and was now half-buried in the strong mud under the root, rolling his left shoulder to ease the discomfort. The robin tried again.

"I don't think the Great Lord will be very happy with your attitude," he declared.

The toad turned his head round very slowly.

"Listen, ugly boy," he said, "your great lord can be as happy or as unhappy as he wants to be. It makes no bloody difference to me."

"You're sure to incur his displeasure," persisted the robin.

"And you're sure to incur my fist up your arse if you don't piss off and leave me alone. I told you: old Arcan will have to wait. I've got things to do."

But the robin, undeterred, plucked up all its courage and played its last card.

"The Great Lord wishes me to inform you that it might be in your interest to answer his summons. He makes particular reference to the condition of your left shoulder . . ."

It let the words tail off and hang there under the toad's nose. The toad nodded glumly. The cunning old bastard, he said to himself. Trust him to know about that. He flexed his shoulder muscles again. The pain was slightly worse. He knew that if anyone could put it right, it was

Arcan. Looks like it's bargaining time again, he thought.

"All right," he said, "tell the old duffer I'm on my way."

The little bird puffed out its chest.

"When may I tell him he is to expect you?" it said, very importantly.

"When I bloody well get there. Now flit off and leave me in peace."

The robin hesitated.

"Piss off, you little bastard!" roared the toad. He made a brief aggressive gesture towards the robin and the little messenger flappered off out of sight without further delay. The toad grunted and settled himself deeper into the mud, pressing his aching shoulder against the underside of the root. But after a while he got up and crawled out into the open.

He moved through the undergrowth in a string of four-footed jumps, keeping to the fresh damp places. A few pieces of sunlight managed to find their way down through the close vegetation, touching the twigs and creepers with a burnt gold light. It was very pretty but the toad didn't care. He only welcomed the tawny glow because it spotlighted the cobwebs and betrayed their spiders to him. More than once he paused on his journey to snatch one and crunch it briskly in his horn-hard mouth.

After one of these mouthfuls he stopped for a while in a small tight spot hemmed-in by a meshwork of hazel stems. The grass underfoot was squelching wet and it reached up over his wrists and paunch. He stood still and enjoyed it. A drab old cranefly passed overhead and he reached out for it with a sudden flick of his enormous tongue. But he missed and could only watch longingly as it drifted out of reach.

Before he was ready to move on, there was a short noise and two beefy young rats came barging their way out of the thicket on the right. Brown rats with lean faces. The toad eyed them with complete disinterest. There were two of them and he had a bad shoulder, so he probably wouldn't be able to eat them. He looked the other way, expecting them to slip off behind him.

The rats, however, had other ideas. They saw at once that he was an outrageously large toad. Easily twice the size of both rats put together. And, young though they were, they knew he wasn't worth eating. They saw the huge skin glands behind the toad's eyes, the smaller warts all over his body, and knew that the fluid inside them was enough to put anybody off. But after all they were rats, and there were other reasons for killing. Although he was a hefty specimen, he was still only a toad . . .

"Who are you then, mister?" said one of them in a thin nasal voice.

The toad was surprised to find them still there. He turned and looked them up and down.

"Ug," he said.

"Ug?" grinned the rat. "Is that your name or are you just clearing your throat?"

They sneezed with laughter. The toad put a smile on his face.

"You're new to the forest, aren't you?" he said.

"That's right," said the other rat. "Came here only yesterday."

The toad nodded.

"I thought so. Thinking of staying, are you?"

The rat shrugged.

"Maybe," it said. "But what's that to you?"

The toad examined his fingers.

"I think you ought to move on," he said confidentially. "Both of you."

"Well, we will. When we've gone to see our mates by the river."

"No, you ought to leave right now."

"Why?"

"Because I say so."

The rats stopped smiling. One of them moved a little closer.

"Oh yes?" it said. "And who the hell are you?"

"You know my name," said Ug dryly. The other rat moved to the shoulder of its colleague. They stood within easy striking distance and their muscles were tight and ready.

"Now then, mister," said one of them, very friendly. "What's all this about? What do you want us to leave for? We ain't hurt nobody."

The toad smiled in their faces.

"Tell you what, lads," he said, equally friendly, "you go back where you came from and learn some respect for those of us who deserve it. Then when you come back you'll be very welcome."

The rats were not amused. They looked at each other, then back at the toad. The one on the left gave a greasy little smile.

"You don't mean that now, do you, mister?"

Ug dropped the smile from his face.

"Bugger off, the pair of you." He said it almost wearily. "I've got things to do and you're getting in my way."

The rat on Ug's left stopped smiling too. Instead it bowed its head as if to ask forgiveness. Its companion did the same. Then suddenly the left-hand rat came up out of its bow with a vicious raking swing of its right arm, aiming for the left side of Ug's face. The toad saw the snarl on the rodent's face and moved his head to get out of the way. He couldn't use his left arm to block the rat's claws because his shoulder was in too much pain. So he whipped his right arm round in a sudden sweeping arc and caught the inside of the rat's wrist in his hand. The follow-through of the same movement flung the young rat over his left shoulder.

The toad's timing was perfect but his strength was abnormal. The rat sailed up over his shoulder and crashed against the trunk of a sloping beech tree. It hit the tree with the nape of its neck, and the force of the collision cracked its spine, three ribs, and a shoulder blade, fractured the base of its skull, and generally killed it before it slid down the treetrunk to the ground.

Ug wasn't looking. As soon as he tossed the rat away, he forgot about it and turned his attention to its partner. The right-hand rat was still staring open-mouthed at the flight of its friend when the toad shot out his hand. The rat squealed and turned sharply away, but Ug caught it by the rump and pulled it back to him. He moved his fingers down and took hold of its long handy tail. Then he held it upside-down in front of him.

For the rat, the sight of Ug's warted face so close to its nose was very unnerving. It had changed its mind about the toad by now, not unnaturally. So much so that it couldn't help pissing itself with fright. The little urine ran hot and quick down its belly.

"Oh, I see," smiled the toad. "Not so brave now, are we?"

The rat couldn't speak.

"You're quite a big little bastard really," said Ug, holding the rat at arm's length to inspect it. "I bet you taste good too." His long thick tongue rushed out of his mouth and stroked the rat's legs. The wretched animal squeaked in terror. Ug drew it back towards him and held it right up against his nose.

"I normally eat little buggers like you for breakfast," he stated. "But this time I'm not going to bother. I'm going to let you go."

The rat couldn't believe its luck.

"Of course," said Ug, "whoever you meet from now on, you'll be sure to tell them you once met the mighty Ug. won't you?"

The rat nodded violently.

"I can't hear you," said the toad.

"Yes!" squealed the rat.

"Good. And you'll let them know that the mighty Ug has to be treated with great respect because he's very delicate and sensitive and his feelings get hurt easily. You'll remember to tell them all that, won't you?"

"Yes, yes!" yelled the rat, almost interrupting him in its eagerness to agree.

"Very good. And of course you'll mention in passing what a remarkably handsome creature the mighty Ug is. Won't you?"

The rat looked at the toad's knobbly brown face and nodded its head.

"Yes!" it cried. "Yes I will!"

"Of course you will. Because it's true, after all. Isn't it?"

"Oh yes!"

"Well done, little shit," said Ug pleasantly. "The right answer every time. Full marks. Now piss off."

And he flicked his hand sideways to the right. The rat

floated away like a flying squirrel, with its limbs splayed out and its teeth in the air. It landed behind a wad of holly in the distance and Ug went on his way. Then he remembered the other rat, the dead one. It seemed a waste to leave it like that. So he jumped over to the beech tree behind him and ate the rat for a while before setting off again. It made a nice change from his usual insect diet.

It was early afternoon by the time Ug the toad finished his journey. The sun had come out and the wet forest had already started to mist. The toad reached the foot of a long grassy slope on the northern edge of the forest, a gradual incline lined with wild cherry trees. Rumour had it that the slope went all the way up to the top of a mountain, out of sight—but Ug didn't know for sure. He'd never been up there himself. Nor did he want to. He stood around and waited. The pain in his shoulder was less sharp than before but the shoulder itself and his left arm were both numb and useless. He reached across with his other hand to rub the aching muscles. And he cursed, as he'd cursed all morning, under his breath.

He went on waiting for a while and when nothing happened he lost his temper.

"Arcan!" he boomed, staring angrily up the damp slope. "Come out here, you old sod—you're wasting my time!"

He heard the last touches of his voice echo off up the hill. A stale leaf dawdled down from one of the cherry trees and a wind blew against Ug's face. A light cold breeze dashing down the slope. It grew stronger. It whipped up a few red leaves and drove them down past the toad as he sat and waited. Then the wind became a small gale, blustering through the bushes and stirring up the branches overhead. Ug narrowed his eyes as the brash air hit him in the face.

And then from the bank of cotton grass that hid the top of the slope there came a flimsy mist. And out of the mist, tall, vivid, and sudden, strode the stately figure of a red deer. A velvet stag, loose-limbed and russet-brown, with a thick ruff of brown hair around his neck. There were a great many points on his wide spreading antlers, which seemed far too heavy for his thin, almost fragile head. He had a tired look on its face, a sad smiling expression. But his eyes were bright as light. When he saw the toad he gave a bow.

"You are very welcome, Ug." The voice was deep but extremely soft.

"Welcome, my arse," said Ug irritably. "Why do you have to keep blasting that wind about every time someone comes to see you? I'm getting a bit tired of your conjuring tricks."

The stag smiled.

"A weakness of mine, I must confess. But also part of a tradition, as you well know."

"Bugger the tradition. Just tell me what you want, then fix my shoulder so I can go home."

"Of course," said the stag. "But first I have something else to ask you."

"Oh yes?" said Ug suspiciously.

"Have no fear," said Arcan. "I only wish to know what happened to the last messengers I sent to you. The two silver dragonflies."

"I ate the bastards," said Ug. The stag sighed and drooped his head.

"Well, what did you expect?" rumbled the toad. "You know I eat insects. And dragonflies are insects."

There was a pale, almost saintly look on the red deer's face. His voice was vaguely sorrowful.

"Is there no way I can persuade you to put aside your cannibalistic habits?"

"What are you talking about?" frowned the toad. "I've never been a cannibal."

"You eat your own kind. Your fellow beings."

"Bollocks," said the toad. "I eat insects. That's what they're here for—to be eaten by us toads."

"Have you ever thought that they, like all creatures, may be here for their own sakes and not for you?"

"No I haven't. Anyway, even if I had, it makes no difference. I'm made that way. I can't help eating insects any more than you can help stuffing yourself with grass and leaves."

"You could learn to eat without killing—"

"No I couldn't. And I don't want to, either. I like the taste of meat too much. Only this morning I had a nice thick piece of brown rat. Lovely it was. All that muscle and sweet red blood—"

"Enough! Please!" said Arcan, in an agonised voice. He took a couple of long strained breaths. "I can see," he added, "that our views on this subject will never be in harmony."

"Then stop trying to change the way I live," said Ug firmly.

The stag nodded his head.

"I wish I could stop," he sighed. "I know it merely serves to keep us apart. But I have to keep trying. It is one of the reasons I am here at all. You understand that, Ug."

The toad looked up into Arcan's large earnest eyes, then looked away.

"Yes," he said. "I understand. But I don't want to go on talking about it all day. Tell me what you want me to do. My shoulder's killing me."

The stag moved closer. He bent his head till his nose was just above Ug's blistered face.

"Does it really hurt you that much?" he asked gently.

"You know bloody well it does!" barked the toad.

The stag nodded again.

"I will soothe your shoulder," he said, and he paused. "When you bring me back my son."

"I haven't got him."

"Do not jest, Ug. This is important. My son is missing."

"Well, you don't need me to find him for you. You can do that yourself."

"I know where he is," said the stag, and he stared at the ground.

"Then go and get him."

Arcan raised his head. There was a look of calm despair in his face.

"He is near the river, Ug," he said limply. "Underground. A prisoner. The rats have taken him."

The toad gave a short deep whistle.

"Oh, shit," he said gravely.

"You can see why I sent for you," said Arcan. "No-one else can save him."

Ug was staring into space.

"I'm not sure even I can do anything for him. If the rats have got him . . ." He shrugged his shoulder.

"Yes," said the stag. And he looked up in the air, high away over the trees. His eyes were wet. "I told him, of course. I warned him not to go near that part of the river in summer. But he rarely listens to me anymore." He stopped and shifted his lips to stop himself from crying.

"Are you sure he's still alive?" said Ug.

"Yes," said the stag. "But he is very weak. The dampness and the black air will soon kill him unless you can reach him first."

The toad looked thoughtful.

"What I don't understand," he said, "is why the bastards didn't kill him right away. I've never heard of rats taking prisoners before."

"Nor I," sighed Arcan. "But, you see, they know who he is. And the son of Arcan is a great prize as a captive. So great, in fact, that they do not know what to do with him. They are not sure if they should kill him now or hold him to ransom. So they wait and do nothing."

"That's very unusual too," mused the toad.

"It is because their leader is not with them."

"Ah!" said Ug. A long drawn-out sigh all to himself. "Now that makes all the difference, that does. The king rat's not there, eh? Is he dead?"

"No," said Arcan. "He will return in a few days. Perhaps even before that."

"Shit," said the toad, "that doesn't leave much time."

He stopped talking and thought furiously for a moment. The red deer looked away across the sky and waited. A roving hedge sparrow flittered past, low in the air. It chirped a brief greeting at the stag and he nodded at it, managed a jaded smile. The wind had died away to nothing.

"No," said Ug, and the stag looked down at him. "I won't do it. It's too dangerous."

Arcan dipped his head. He appeared to be staring down at his own knees and his antlers hovered over the toad's head.

"He is my only son," said the High Stag. "The others are all dead. If he dies with them, our whole line is extinguished."

"I can't help that," gruffed the toad. "It's not my fault the little fool got himself caught."

"But you can set him free." The stag looked up and there was excitement in his eyes. "You have the strength of the ages in your body, and the stature to penetrate their den in secret. Will you really not help us?"

"I told you," said Ug. "It's too bloody dangerous. There are hundreds of those bastard rats and only one of me. It's too much of a risk."

"If my son dies, you know what will happen. The balance of the forest will be destroyed."

"Crap."

"You know it is the truth. You know our line must survive if the forest is to survive. Without me—without my son—there is only you, Ug. And your strength alone can only do so much. You must free my son."

"I won't."

"For the balance of the forest, you must set him free."

"The balance?" snarled the toad, and he spat at the red deer's feet. "What will I care about the balance if I'm torn to pieces by those bloody rats? Bugger the balance. Bugger the whole forest for all I care. I'm not killing myself for anybody."

The silence that followed was filled only by the creaking of the High Stag's antlers as he shook his head very slowly from side to side. He looked down and gazed at the toad.

"And what of your shoulder?" said the deep satin voice.

The toad flexed his arm. The shoulder muscles hissed with pain and he couldn't stop himself wincing. Arcan nodded his head.

"The pain is still there," he said quietly. "It has not left you quickly this time."

"It'll be all right," mumbled Ug. "It always clears up in the end."

"Yes, I know. But each time it stays a little longer. Each time it pains you a little more."

The toad just grunted.

"It will kill you, Ug."

"Balls," said the toad, as expected.

"Each time it returns it draws the power from your arm. Soon you will not be able to use the arm. And then the pain will spread, Ug. Across your back to the other arm. Before long both your arms will die and you will be able to catch nothing. Then all you can do is sit and wait for death, wait for the greenbottle fly to deposit her eggs on your neck and the young maggots to slide in through your nostrils to eat your brains, your eyes—"

"Oh, shut up!" groaned the toad. "I don't want to hear all that."

"That is the way it must be," said Arcan very seriously, shaking his venerable head. Ug was breathing hard. There was a scowl on his face.

"Find my son, Ug," said the stag. "Find him and bring him back to me. Then I will heal your shoulder and it will never trouble you again."

The toad puffed out his cheeks and gulped once or twice. It looked as if he was trying to swallow his eyes.

"All right," he said. "Looks like I've got no choice. But I can't do it in the state I'm in. You'll have to do something about this bloody shoulder first."

"At once," said Arcan, and he lowered his head. "Reach up," he said. "Touch my horns with your hand."

The toad lifted his arm.

"No," said the deer. "The other one."

"I can't bloody move it."

"Reach up," said Arcan, and his voice was stronger. The toad stretched his left arm with difficulty. He closed his thick fingers round a point on one of the antlers and held on.

"Take your hand away."

He did.

"How does it feel?"

He jerked the shoulder backwards and forwards and rolled his arm.

"Good," he said. "Not bad, anyway. It's still a bit stiff."

"And so it shall be—until you return with my son. Then I shall heal it completely."

"You mean you've left it like this deliberately?" There was profound surprise in the toad's voice. "What's the matter—you trust me, don't you?"

Arcan sighed.

"Ug," he said quietly, "we are not the same, you and I. That is both good and bad for the forest. But at times like these we must have a point of contact. And since you will not adjust your character to meet mine, I must adapt mine to meet yours. Thus I am forced to bargain with you. I use a fragment of your own wariness. It is not something I wish to do, as you know—but there are great things at stake."

"Shit," breathed the toad. "Never use one word when three or four will do, eh? You never bloody change, do you?"

"I am not a wind, Ug. I am not made to change. I am as constant as you yourself."

"All right, all right," said Ug. "Just tell me where they're keeping that son of yours and I'll be on my way."

The stag looked away to the south.

"Down by the Great River," he said. "In a large chamber of earth. There is a narrow tunnel that opens on the riverbank by the last line of white willows."

"Right," said Ug grimly. He turned and hopped off away from the green slope. "You'd better hope I make it, soft-head," he called out over his shoulder. "Otherwise we've all had it. Me, you, your idiot son, and this precious forest of yours. Wish me luck."

Arcan had it in mind to tell him there was no such thing as luck, but he kept it to himself. Instead he said nothing —and as the restored toad jumped away to the south, he turned and cantered fluidly up the slope and out of sight behind the cotton grass. A slapstick wind came out to play with the leaves and follow him up the hill.

The main forest river slid past a cluster of white willows like a flow of green milk, fat and full of fish. Many of the willow roots were exposed as they dipped into the water, and between two of these roots was a small hole dug into the crumbling riverbank, half hidden by slack mud and tree fibres. Out onto the lip of the hole came a brown rat, followed by two others. They stood and looked up and down the river, examined the far bank and the tree above them. Their faces were thin and their eyes small and suspicious.

"I still think you're overdoing it," said one of them.

"I'm just making sure," said another.

"Well, I agree with Gripe," said the third. "There's no need for all this."

"That's right," said the first rat. "We can keep a look-out just as well inside as out here."

The second rat snorted and went on studying the thick grass on the far side of the river.

"Maybe you're right," he shrugged. "It all looks quiet enough."

"Let's go back in then," said Gripe.

"All right. But we'll come out and have a look round every half-hour. If some bugger does get inside, it's my head that gets bitten off."

"What are you so worried about?" asked the third rat. "No-one's going to risk paying this place a visit."

"I don't know about that," muttered rat number two, glancing apprehensively up the river. "There's that big bastard stoat for a start."

"What, him? No, he's dead. The old pike got him."

"Eh?" said the other. "Are you sure?"

" 'Course I'm sure. They killed each other. That little vole told me himself."

"Ah," said the second rat. But Gripe wasn't interested.

"Come on," he growled. "Let's get back inside. It's too bloody bright out here."

They turned and scuttled out of sight. From behind a wedge of sweet-grass on the other bank, Ug the toad watched them disappear and licked his cheek, deep in thought.

He knew now that Arcan had been telling the truth. It had occurred to him that the old stag's son might not have been underground at all, that he, the toad, had simply been sent to his death. But the sight of these rats guarding the black hole convinced him that the young deer was indeed their prisoner. He'd never known the rats to guard their fortress so carefully. They clearly knew the value of their captive and feared some kind of reaction from the High Stag.

He hopped away to the right and bulled his way through the sweet-grass before slipping down into the river itself. He made his way across to the other side with slow and silent, almost graceful strokes. Then out of the water, up the bank and across to the rat hole. He hid for a moment behind a thin grey willow root, then picked a handful of soft mud out of the bank. He flung the mud hard and loud into the water below the hole and waited for the sentries to come running. They didn't. He knew then that no-one in the rat colony really believed the young deer could be rescued. They weren't worried or alert enough. And that was a good sign.

He jumped into the mouth of the hole and down the thin black passage. The smell of dung and decay hit him in the face and the tunnel was a very tight fit. He knew they couldn't have dragged old Arcan's son in through here. They must have used a much wider entrance, probably nearer the forest. And that meant he would have to go deep into the garrison to find him.

Soon the dark passage divided into three, a complication Ug could have done without. He stopped to think for a moment, then made up his mind and hid himself in the shadow of one of the corner walls. He muscled his back and hindquarters against the soil to form a rough alcove for himself. And he kept his eyes half-shut to stop them gleaming in the dark. Then he waited.

The first rats to pass by were sleek and slant-eyed. There were too many of them, so Ug left them alone. Then he saw another group coming his way. Three of them. Not too bad. He knew he would have to move fast, and he did. Before they knew what was happening, two of the rats were dead, their skulls crushed like eggs under Ug's sledgehammer fists. The other had a short second in which to squeal or run, but it was too terrified. The toad grabbed it, the whole of it in one hand, and held it in front of his face, two fingers keeping its mouth firmly shut.

"Now then, dirty boy," he whispered. "You're going to do me a good turn, you are."

He stopped talking when he heard the sound of footsteps, and pressed himself back into his little corner with the rat clutched tightly to his breastbone. A small patrol of rats passed by. Six or seven of them. They saw the dead bodies of their two associates and started gibbering amongst themselves, looking around with fear in their faces. They didn't see the toad. They dragged the two corpses off by their tails and vanished down one of the dark tunnels. Ug waited till they were gone, then lifted up his rat and poked it in the chest with his finger.

"Listen here, you," he hissed. "I've got no time to waste, so be a good boy and tell me where the young deer is. When I take my fingers away, tell me where they're keeping him, quick and clear. No lies and no screaming or I'll lift your throat out. Got it? Right then."

He released the rat's jaw and it gulped.

"In the wide room," it gasped. "Down the passage on the left. The big room on the right at the end. It's a long way down." Its mouth clapped shut and Ug nodded in approval.

"Very good, dirty boy," he said. "You'll go far, you will."

He crushed its head in his hand and hopped off up the left-hand corridor.

It was a long passageway, much wider than the one he left behind. Ten times as wide. There were shadows everywhere, and thin bearded roots poking through the soil walls. Plenty of places to hide.

He'd expected this particular gallery to be crawling with rats by now, and he was right. The whole colony seemed to be there up ahead of him, knowing that two of their number had been killed.

"How do you know they weren't just killed in a brawl or something?" asked a fat rat with no tail. His neighbour shuddered.

"No," he said. "You should've seen their heads. All smashed-in and flat. There's no rat could do something like that."

"Not even the king?"

"Well, he's not back yet. But no, not even him."

"What then? A badger maybe?"

"When was the last time you seen a badger down here? No, they never—hey, what's that?"

"Where?"

What the rat had seen was the body of another rat falling out of the shadows and lying nice and still on the ground. It was quite dead. Its head had been wrenched off. The nearest rat saw it and screamed. But it was a warning call, not a cry of terror. In seconds the broad corridor was absolutely filled with rats, running in from all over the place. Each one wanted to examine the headless body closely—and, as planned, Ug the toad took advantage of the general confusion to creep unnoticed along the wall, hidden by hanging roots.

"The deer!" someone shouted. "Stay close to the wide room!"

Some of them didn't move. Others began searching the

walls. And a large herd of them rushed off to the far end of the passage. There they stopped and congregated in front of a wide opening already guarded by a dozen of the heaviest rats.

"Now what?" grunted the head guard.

"It's in here, whatever it is. It's just killed another of my boys. Looks like it's after the young stag."

"Shit," said the guard. "What is it—does anybody know?"

"No idea. But it's bloody strong and it's getting closer. I brought some reinforcements."

"Good," said the guard. "Looks like we're going to need them."

The reinforcements were bad news for the toad. He was crouched behind a root that reached from the ceiling of the tunnel down into the floor. A kind of natural pillar. And he was almost directly opposite the large chamber itself. But now it was defended by more rats than he could cope with—and there were more of them arriving every second.

"Search the walls!" cried a long thin rat who appeared to be in charge. "Dig around in the dirt if you have to. I want the bastard found before he gets too close."

The rats did as they were told. Ug heard them feeling their way along the wall towards him, moving in from both sides. He knew it was hopeless trying to hide much longer. He would have to gamble on a show of force. He looked out round the side of the root. There must have been a hundred of them out there, waiting, on edge, their eyes glancing left and right, their noses sniffing at the air. Just then, one of the search parties reached the wall behind Ug's pillar—and one of the rats spotted him. He turned and saw it—but before he could act, it had darted out across the tunnel, squealing like a rabbit.

"It's here, it's here!" it yelled. "I seen it!"

The rats went mad. Leaping and scuffling all over each other. Their long thin leader screamed and cursed at them to keep order—and then the giant toad made his move and hopped out from behind his root.

There was almost instant silence as they all turned and stared at him. Some of them had seen him before and all of them knew him by reputation. Although there were a hundred or more of them gathered outside the dark wide room, none of them felt very comfortable as they faced him. In that crowded space he looked even bigger than usual, and each rat felt it was facing him alone. One small rodent was so transfixed by him that it failed to back off as quickly as the others. And the toad snatched it up like an acorn. He held it high in the air in one hand and pushed out his chest. His voice seemed to make the whole tunnel shiver.

"Here I am, sons of shit!" He used the rat in his hand to point at the dark opening behind them. "I want that young buck you've got in there and I'm going to take him—even if I have to break all your bones to do it!"

He threw the rat over their heads and it thumped into the dirt wall at huge speed. Half its body was driven into the soil and its hindquarters stuck out of the wall at right angles. The army of rats screeched in horror—and Ug jumped in on them before they had time to recover, scattering them with his fists. For a moment there was wholesale panic among the rats. Those who weren't smashed aside ran of their own accord, tumbling and screaming down the passage. But then over the bedlam came the voice of the long thin rat, desperate but loud and clear.

"Stand together, you bits of crap! There's only one of him! Stand and fight or I'll chew all your heads off myself!"

The words were defiant enough, but they didn't work. The rats ran left right and centre fighting one another to get out of the way. Ug felt a thrill in his chest as he realised it was all going to work. He went on marching through the rats towards the wide room, crushing their heads in his mouth and fingers. The little scavengers had no answer to him.

"Stand together, I said!" screamed the leader rat. "You can run now but you won't escape the king rat when he finds out about this. Stand together—stand and fight!"

The king rat! The words punched into the chest of every one of them. Nothing—not even the toad's utter strength—could throw as much terror into the brain of a brown rat. The killer king! He would be back soon. They all knew that however hard they ran now, there was nowhere to hide from the fury of the king. Those who were running away came back. Those who were still standing hesitating in front of the doorway leapt forward to confront the toad. At first he spread their brains across the floor, but then they began to attack from all sides, from behind him, raking his back with their claws, biting at least once before he split their heads open. Soon there were so many of them that they were hanging from his arms and covering his head with their bodies. He felt them hugging on to his mouth and nostrils to stop his breathing, and he pulled them away. But there were others scrambling to take their places, and even his great muscles began to tire with the effort of keeping them at bay. He released the harsh fluid from his skin glands but it made no difference. They bit his legs and feet until he was forced to fall on his side. Then they pinned him there by sheer weight of numbers, gnawing at his thick cold flesh.

"That's enough!" cried the leader rat. "Get your paws off him. I want the king rat to see him alive."

The rats hissed and muttered among themselves.

"You're mad!" said one. "He's too dangerous to keep alive. He'll kill us all!"

The others howled in agreement.

"No!" said the leader. "He'll be safe enough. Tear the skin off his back and break his arms!"

There was a loud anguished howl from the toad and he struggled to get up. They held him down.

"Break his arms and legs and dump him in the wide room!"

The rats approved of this. They did what they were told and Ug's struggles were useless. They pulled back his limbs and dislocated the main joints one by one, giggling with glee each time he roared with the pain. Then they peeled the skin off his body, fighting each other for the bigger strips. Some of them still wanted to kill him, but the leader rat overruled them.

"Drag him into the wide room and leave him there. He won't be leaving us."

They heaved the huge skinless body through the dark opening and left him in the back of the room.

"Snag," said the leader rat. The head guard appeared at his side. "Leave two dozen of your boys outside. That should be enough."

Snag nodded and moved away.

"The rest of you piss off back to what you were doing before. The king rat's back any time after tomorrow and I want the place ready for him."

The rats scuttled away and left only the two dozen guards behind them. The old familiar silence returned, and time passed slowly for those outside the wide room . . .

Ug was hunched against the far wall of the dark chamber. They'd dumped him behind a mound of earth, out of sight, leaving him to feel the pains in his body. Every joint was torn and useless, but his bones had been left unbroken. He didn't try to move his legs.

When he heard something creeping around beside him he thought it was a rat. Then he remembered he was in the room where they were keeping Arcan's son, and he thought that was who it was. But it was too small.

"Who are you?" he murmured. The little creature stopped moving about.

"It's only me, sir," it said in a high quiet voice. "Vim the vole, sir. You don't know me."

The toad grunted.

"Is there anything I can do to help, sir?"

Ug looked at the vole. It had moved round directly in front of him.

"No," he said. "You're too small."

Vim looked sad. It was true. He was too small.

"What have they done to you, sir?"

"Pulled my limbs out of joint, the bastards. Torn the skin off me."

"Oh dear," said the vole. Ug half-smiled.

"It could have been worse," he said. "I always shed my skin this time of year, so that didn't matter. I usually eat it too—but they got it this time."

The vole nodded and licked his nose.

"Where's the young buck?" said the toad.

"The little lord?" said Vim brightly. "Why, he's over there, sir. At the other end of the room. Shall I lead you to him?"

"I can't move, you moron."

"Oh no, of course not. Forgive me, sir. I'll go and fetch him. But it might take a little time. He's not been feeling too well, you see."

The vole turned to go but Ug called him back.

"Why are you still alive?" he asked suspiciously. "I can understand them not killing the stag, but you're no use to them."

Vim coughed.

"Well, you see, sir . . . I don't think these rats are all that clever. They caught me about the same time as the young lord, and when they decided to keep him alive they just decided to leave me alone too. I'm no use to them, as you say—but I hope they don't find that out in a hurry!"

The toad was satisfied with that.

"All right," he said. "Go and fetch that buck over here."

The vole skuddered across the floor, leaving Ug to wonder why Arcan's son hadn't said a word so far. The little idiot's probably dead, he thought. Just my luck.

He heard the sound of something scuffling towards him. And a wheezing noise punctuated by squeaks of encouragement from the vole. There was enough noise to attract the head guard's attention, and he came sneaking into the chamber.

"What's all this?" he said. "Where are you two going?"

"I'm helping the young lord across the room," said Vim. "He and the toad are going to talk for a while. That's all."

The rat eyed them for a moment.

"All right," he sniffed. "No harm in that, I suppose. But any clever business and I'll bite your balls off, vole. Just you remember that."

"Yes I will," said Vim courteously. Snag left the room.

"Here he is, lord," said the vole. "The great toad who fought to reach you. He's badly wounded. Perhaps you can help him."

Ug looked at the young deer. It was lying breathing hard with its chest on the ground and its forelegs out in front of it. The antlers were mere stumps on its head and the face was that of its father. But the eyes were bolder.

"Can you do anything for me, whelp?" said Ug. "Has your father taught you that much?"

"He has taught me more than that," said the deer. The voice was thin as silk. "But first I would know what to call you."

"Ug."

"Your bravery and strength are fine things, brother Ug. But I do not know why you are here."

"Your father sent me to get you out."

"Ah!" The deer nodded its head. "It is as I thought. And my father told you I was a captive, a hostage of the brown rats, did he not?"

"That's right."

"My father has lied to you, Ug."

The toad's eyes opened wide, then half-closed.

"No," he said. "Arcan doesn't lie. He might make mistakes, but he's no liar."

The stag looked him full in the face.

"My father, Ug, is lord of the forest. He knows all things. He cannot make mistakes."

He paused. Ug knew he was right.

"He has lied to you, Ug. I am not a prisoner of these good rats."

"Good rats?" frowned the toad. "They pulled my bloody legs out of place."

"I know," sighed the deer. "It was very extreme of them. But all things must be true to their nature."

"Never mind that," said Ug. "Are you trying to tell me you weren't captured by these little shits?"

"I was not."

"So you came here by yourself? What the hell for?"

The deer took a deep breath.

"My father, Ug, is a dreamer. He is lord of the forest but lord only in spirit. I am different. I wish to be a real lord."

"And you think these little cut-throats are going to help you?"

"Yes. They have promised to make me their king."

"What?" The toad couldn't believe he was hearing all this. "And you believed them? It's you that's the dreamer, boy. They'll kill you."

"No. They have promised."

"Sod it, child—these are rats, not roebucks. You said yourself they're true to their nature. And their nature is to kill. Have they fed you?"

"They are waiting until their chieftain returns. He will feed me. And make me king."

"Instead of himself, I suppose? They're saving you for him, can't you see that? He's as big as me, almost as strong, and twice as vicious. If he doesn't eat you at once, he'll use you against your father and kill you later."

"I do not believe that."

"Your head's full of shit, boy. But there's still time. We can get out of this place."

"I will not."

"We're both dead if you don't."

"No!" said the deer, in a fuller voice. "I will be king. I will! I will not return to be my father's trained mouse. And do not forget, Ug, that he has lied to you. He has used you. You owe him nothing."

The toad scowled at the floor. It was true enough. The old stag had taken him for a ride. He didn't like that. He could pay the old fraud back by leaving his son to the rats. He looked up.

"It makes no difference, boy. Only your father can fix my shoulder. And he won't do it unless I take you back to him. So you're coming with me."

"You are helpless, toad. You cannot take me any-where."

"Then help me, lad. Make me strong again and I'll get us both out of here. It's the only chance we've got left."

"I shall take my chance with the chief rat."

There was no more to be said. It was time, Ug knew, to take drastic measures. Although his arms and legs were out of action, the rest of him was still strong. And Arcan's son was close enough. With one massive jerk of his neck and trunk he drove his head under the young buck's chin and closed his mouth in the soft neck. He could feel the windpipe as he held on.

"No!" gasped the deer. "What are you doing?"

"Not so loud, little boy," hissed the toad through clenched teeth. "If those rats outside hear you, I'm dead. And so are you."

"If you kill me, you'll never get out of here," wailed the deer, in a softer voice.

"I've got nothing to lose," said Ug. "You're my only

chance of getting away and if you don't help me I'd just as soon kill you as not."

"But how can I help?"

"You know bloody well. Make me strong. Put my joints back into shape. I'll do the rest."

"No!" said the deer, but Ug wasn't taking that for an answer.

"I mean it, boy. Mend my arms and legs or I'll pluck your dainty little throat out."

By way of encouragement, he clenched his teeth a shade tighter. The young deer sucked in his breath. He lifted a spindly leg and touched each of the toad's limbs with his hoof. Ug heard him murmuring something. Then the hoof went away. The toad flexed his arms and thrilled to find them healed, heaving with power. The left shoulder was still sore, but he'd expected that. Only Arcan himself could heal it.

"Good boy!" he breathed. "Now then, roll yourself over into that corner, behind the big root."

The deer didn't argue. He crawled sulkily across the floor.

"And you, little piddler, go and join him."

The vole obeyed at once.

"That's good," said Ug. "Now, Vim my lad, when I give the sign, you squeak your head off, see? I want those bastards out there to come running in like the plague."

He moved noiselessly to the doorway. The rats were all arranged in small groups just outside. They had their backs to the room and didn't see him as he took up a position to the right of the entrance. He looked round and nodded to the vole.

"Help!" he squealed. "Ow! Help! The toad, the toad!"

The rats came pouring in at once, all of them. They raced across the room and found the deer and the vole alone behind the root.

"What's going on?" growled Snag. "Where's that toad gone?"

Ug answered his question with a laugh. The rats turned round and saw his huge bulk blocking the doorway. He didn't say anything, just beckoned to them with his forefinger and smiled.

The sight of the toad drove the rats wild with panic. There was no question of any tactical manoeuvring. They ran blindly around the room looking for another doorway. But there was only one. Some of them rushed towards it. They died very quickly. And the others didn't last long. One or two chose to fight their way out, another tried to sneak past unseen. The toad pulled their heads off.

When all the rats were dead, Ug counted them. They were all there. Not one had escaped to raise the alarm.

"Well, that's that," he said. "Vim my boy, where's the nearest way out?"

"Down the passage on the right," said the vole. "But most of the rats are around there and it won't be big enough for the young lord. There is another way. It's longer, but safer and wider."

"Good. You can lead us to it. I'll have to drag our friend along myself. He's too weak to move very far."

He jumped over to the young stag and took hold of his hind leg. But the deer kicked his hand away.

"I am not going back," he said feebly.

"We'll see about that," said Ug, less feebly.

"Leave me!" wailed the buck. "You're no different from the rats with all your killing. And I hate my father. I won't go back."

The toad had no time for this.

"Listen, you," he said. "If I don't take you back, old Arcan won't fix my shoulder, see? And if that happens, I'm up the creek. So, one way or another, I'm taking you back. Since I've got to drag you anyway, I'll be quite happy to put you to sleep before I do. Unless you behave yourself."

The deer pouted but said nothing. Ug picked up its hind leg again. There was no resistance this time. He turned round, put the leg on his shoulder, and pulled the thin grey body out of the room. Then with Vim leading the way he hustled off along the corridor, going left.

It was tiring work for the toad, but at least no-one got in the way. They did bump into one small round rat, but Ug ate him. At last they reached a point where the corridor turned sharply uphill. At the top of the hill they saw a point of light. The way out. Ug was as relieved as the vole, but he was also very tired. And his left shoulder was throbbing with pain. There was nothing the young stag could have done to soothe it, even if he'd wanted to, so Ug just had to go on as he was. And with every step he expected to hear sounds of pursuit behind them. The rats must surely have discovered they were gone by now.

He heaved the deer up the crumbling slope. The vole was too small to help him, but he made himself useful by keeping watch behind them. Just when Ug thought his strength was going to run out, they reached the top of the hill. The floor levelled out and the pale sunlight was at the end of a large earthen hallway. They could hear the sound of the river creeping along outside. Ug stopped for a quick rest, breathing hard. He was just beginning to wonder how he could force Arcan's son to walk unaided when something totally unexpected happened to him. He was attacked by a rat.

It was quite alone as it dropped down from the tunnel ceiling, where it had been hiding on a hanging root. When it landed on his shoulders, Ug swung at it with his hand. But the rat knew what it was doing. It dug its claws into the skin just above his waist and hung on, biting at his spine. The toad turned and twisted but couldn't shake it off. He was hit by a feeling of immense fatigue and his shoulder was just a piece of pain. The rat bit a chunk out of his back.

"Remember me?" it hissed. "You killed my mate in the woods. And you threw me over that hedge. I've been following you . . ."

It clambered up his neck and slashed his head with its claws. The pain was very faint. Ug had no strength left and he fell to the ground. He heard the vole squealing something about the rats coming closer, but it was all too late, too far away. The rat was tearing at his face now, laughing, knowing it had won. He looked at the young stag but it wasn't going to help him. There was blood in his nostrils and the deer was just watching . . .

Then, quite suddenly, the rat fell off. Ug looked across and saw it scrambling about in the dirt. The little vole had dragged it off him. The rat was by Ug's side. It was getting up to punish the vole. With the last of his strength the toad put his hand round it and squeezed. At last one of its eyes burst open and blood seeped from its nose. He let it fall.

"Good work, little runt," he said to the vole. Vim tugged at his fingers.

"The rats!" he cried. "The rats are coming! Can't you hear them?"

The toad got up slowly. He could hear them now. He lifted his head and saw them. They were at the foot of the long tunnel slope. The long thin rat was at their head. Hundreds of them. The end of the world.

"Come on," he panted, grabbing at the red deer's hoof. "You can get out yourself now."

"No!" said the stag. "I stay here. I will be king."

"You'll be dead, that's all. We'll all be dead, curse you. Come on."

"No! I stay!"

The rats were rushing up the hill. The long thin leader urged them on.

"There they are!" he yelled. "Get after them, all of you! They're food for the king. If they get away he'll feed on us instead of them!"

"There!" said the toad. "You heard that. Look at them all coming after you. Do you still want to stay and meet their king?"

The young buck gave a quick high-pitched moan and started to drag itself out of the tunnel into the open air. Ug could do no more than hang on to its hind leg and let himself be towed along. The vole brought up the rear.

When they were out of the hole, the stag got up very awkwardly and lowered its head for the toad to hop onto its neck. Vim jumped up behind him. Then they were away, the stag finding some of its natural speed to bound away from the rat hole. They left it far behind and didn't hear the sharp cursing voices of the thousand rats robbed of their prey. Only the long thin leader didn't speak. He watched the young deer leaping away along the riverbank and his teeth chattered nervously. It was he who would have to answer to the king rat . . .

The three fugitives were in Arcan's country now. The stag stopped among the cherry trees near the foot of the green slope. There they waited.

"Ug," said the deer, in a quiet voice, "I have caused you much suffering. I am sorry."

The toad grunted.

"I have been a fool."

"True," said Ug.

"Worse than that, I have flirted with evil. I did not fully restore your strength in that black room."

Ug said nothing. He wasn't surprised.

"Your strength is truly a wondrous thing. And your bravery shall not be forgotten. I hope you can forgive me."

The toad looked the other way.

"I have listened to the wrong thoughts," said the buck. "But I am changed now. I only pray my father can forgive me in his heart."

"So long as he does my shoulder and patches me up, I don't give a rat's arse," said Ug.

The wind started to sweep down the hill again. Another mist grew out of the cotton grass. And the lord of the forest rode down to meet them with a strolling of hooves and a sway of his antlers.

"Be welcome!" he cried, in a joyful voice. His son hung his head—and that threw the vole off his shoulders. Ug tumbled off with a curse. The great stag bowed very low.

"Well done, little vole of courage!" he said. "You will always be in my thoughts." Vim didn't speak or look up, but his heart was beating very fast and his eyes were shining.

"And you, my son . . ."

The buck lifted his head.

"Father—"

"No," said the High Stag, very gently. "All is forgiven and all is well. All is very well."

"The hell it is!" The toad was lying in a heap. His face and body were blotched with drying blood. Half his face seemed to be hanging off.

"What about my bastard shoulder?" he huffed.

Arcan wasted no time. He bent and breathed hard all over the toad's body, licked the wounds with his heavy tongue. When he'd finished, Ug was as good as new. There was a scowl on his face.

"You lied to me, old one." The voice was slow, even deeper than usual. Arcan knew he was treading on thin ice.

"Yes," he said gravely. "But it was the only way to save my son."

"I don't care about all that. No-one lies to me. I don't like being used." He took a jump forward and fixed his hot red eyes on the old stag. Arcan looked down at him and opened his mouth—but even he was lost for words.

"I nearly got myself killed because you lied to me. I don't like that."

He hopped closer and stood right underneath the lord of the forest. His throat and biceps were twitching and pumping, the veins on his forearms like fingers of ivy, and Arcan knew the toad had murder in mind. But he stood his ground. His son and the vole stood still and helpless to one side.

"I only did as you would have done, Ug." His voice was calm enough. "And, after all, I have upheld my side of the agreement. Your shoulder is healed. Forever."

Ug didn't answer. He leaned back slightly and his muscles were taut, ready to spring. He rolled his shoulders.

"Well," he said slowly, "I can't deny that." He nodded thoughtfully. "All right, old one. You and your brat can live. But if you trick me like that just once more I'll feed your heads to the crows." Then he smiled and puffed out his enormous chest. "Well, at least I'm back to full strength. Back to my old beautiful self."

The others smiled. None of them laughed.

"I sometimes wonder, Ug," said Arcan, "if you do not perhaps care a little too much for your own appearance."

"Well, let's face it," said the toad, "what else have I got except my strength and my good looks?"

There was no answer to that.

"And now, little warrior," said Arcan to the vole, "it would be as well for you to return home at once."

"Yes, lord," said Vim. "But why at once?"

"Because, my son, now that the mighty Ug has recovered his strength, he has also rediscovered his appetite."

The vole looked at the toad. The toad looked at the vole. And Vim ran off as fast as he could without another word.

Ug turned and jumped away across the grass.

"Stay with us awhile," said Arcan. "We have much to talk about, you and I."

"We've got nothing to say to each other," retorted Ug.

"Then allow me to thank you," said the stag. "For myself, my son, and the forest."

The toad nodded brusquely.

"Yes, well . . . anyway, I've had a bellyful of all this," he said. "I'm going home."

"Will you not stay, even for a short time?"

"No. I've got better things to do." Then he grinned.

"And anyway, who wants to stay here with you ugly bastards?"

And he jumped away towards the forest. The two stags watched him go, then trotted up the grassy slope, very close together. The wind followed them and disappeared.

OLD
COMMON

FIRST LIGHT ON A CHILL EARLY
winter day. A set of bending grass hills just beyond
the forest, split into fields by a crosswork of gorse bushes.
A brook running out of the forest across the fields. A damp
morning mist and a rain.

Under the foot of a gorse bush, eyes and ears wide open
in the grim light, lay Old Common the hare, watching and
waiting. His body was fitted into the base of the bush and
his ears were flat on his neck. Only his nose was out,
sniffing at the drizzle. His eyes, set round in the side of his
head, gave him a wide view of the field that sloped up
away from him to the grey horizon. The forest was across
to his left but he couldn't see it. At the moment there was
only the field and the rain and he went on waiting.

He'd been there since just before dawn, crouched and
ready, his plans already made. Now it was only a matter
of time.

Then over the freckling of the rain in the gorse there was another sound. More than one. They came from where he'd expected them, from behind the hill in front of him. The ground shivered very faintly under the distant tread of boots and paws. The air brought him the sound of a few gruff commands. And above all that, the strong sharp yapping of two dogs.

The ears of the hare were twitching and his pulse was loud and restless, but everything was under control. The dogs were on time and the weather was perfect. He smiled. It was going to be another easy day.

The noises were louder now. When they reached the right volume, the hare sprang out of his hiding place and charged off up the hill. A third of the way up, he suddenly took off in a huge sideways leap to the right. Then he ran on a few paces and jumped again, moving off even further to the right. After that he dashed up the slope and hid in another gorse bush halfway up the hill.

He looked out and waited. The bush he'd run out of was away at the bottom of the hill on his left, but he wasn't looking at that. His eyes were on the wide space between the bushes at the crown of the slope, high up on his right. The distant sounds grew louder. The bushes rustled behind the top of the field. The hare wiped his nose on his shoulder. And in a welter of barking and gasping two muscular dogs raced out of the mist and careered down the green hill.

Old Common almost frowned when he saw them. Just the two of them, as usual. But not the old familiar dogs. One was a greyhound, bone-thin and grey, legs like reeds. The other was more heavily built, thicker in the jaw. A brindled lurcher. They looked altogether more menacing than the scrawny fleabags that were normally sent out after the hare. The lurcher in particular looked very strong and deep-chested. It wouldn't tire easily. And Old Common wasn't getting any younger.

Still, as he watched the dogs rush downhill, he knew he could still lead them a bit of a dance. Like all the others, they were soon confused when they picked up his scent near the foot of the hill. They followed it down to the gorse bush at the bottom, then came back up when they found nothing there. When they reached the point where Old Common had jumped to one side, they stopped. The scent was lost. It was a hare's first and most elementary trick, and in the thick wet air there was little hope of picking up his trail.

But these were uncommon dogs. The lurcher moved away sharply to the left and found nothing, but it wasn't bothered. It ran back and across to the right, where it found the waiting scent and followed it at once, the greyhound moving along behind him, trotting up the slope to the spot where the hare had made his second leap. This time they worked as a pair. The lurcher went off to the left again and the greyhound sniffed away to the right, where it found Old Common's trail in no time.

The hiding hare saw them coming across the grass towards him and knew he had to do something pretty quickly. But he was still unconcerned. There were other tricks in his head. When the dogs were quite close, he broke cover and let them see him as he shot away along the side of the gorse bush, going downhill. As soon as they spotted him, the dogs broke into a sprint—but they never even looked like catching him. He was gone, his off-white tail disappearing through a gap in the dense bush.

There seemed no hole wide enough for the dogs, but they took that in their stride. One moved away to the left, the other to the right, nosing at the bush with impressive patience. The lurcher barked. It had found a way through.

The field on the other side was the hare's second ploy. It was a short broad meadow dipping down to the brook, well-grassed and marshy. The dogs found the watery mud reaching up over their ankles. The hare, of course, was nowhere in sight, so they would have to hunt him by smell again—and the sodden ground wasn't there to help them.

So they changed their tactics. Instead of sniffing about in the grass they ran down towards the lumps of gorse at the bottom of the field, knowing the hare couldn't be very far away. It was a straightforward thing to do, simple and direct—but it took Old Common by surprise. He was lying watching under a small holly bush at the foot of the meadow, and he wasn't at all pleased to see the dogs simply ignoring his second line of defence. Their prompt action had taken away any time for leisurely thinking. He had to act fast.

The dogs didn't know exactly where he was hiding, so they split up to look for him. The greyhound came down the left-hand side of the field, the lurcher down the right. Old Common waited till they'd almost reached the gorse bushes then he took off at full speed and hurtled back up the rain-soaked hill, veering to the left. The dogs saw him, shouted and gave chase—but he dodged up the slope and vanished down the mouth of a burrow in the shadows of yet another block of gorse.

It was an old familiar bolt-hole. It had another exit and it gave him the chance to take a breather. He pushed his way down the tunnel, reached the wide chamber at the end of it and—oh shit, there was a fox in the burrow.

It was just lying there, looking very comfortable with its nose between its front paws. The gasping hare held his breath. He couldn't believe his luck. First the dogs and now this. Out of the forest fire into the snare.

The fox lifted its head. It looked him up and down and smiled.

"Well, hello," it drawled. "How nice of you to drop in."

The hare started breathing again. His face relaxed and he nodded at the fox.

"Hello, Norris," he panted. "How are you?"

The fox shrugged an elegant shoulder.

"Oh, not bad, old chap. Touch of old age, perhaps, but nothing serious."

The hare nodded again. His breathing was a little more even. He looked at the fox and was quietly thankful it was only old toothless Norris. He hadn't recognised him at first.

"I say, old man," said the fox, "you look a bit out of puff. Been for a stroll, have you?"

Old Common shook his head.

"Dogs." It was all he needed to say. Norris understood these things.

"Oh, I see," sniffed the fox. "How very boring for you. Still, I suppose it's one way of passing the time."

"No," said the hare. "These two are different. They know what they're doing."

"Impossible."

"It's true, I'm afraid."

"But, my dear chap, we both know that the peasants they send out after us are only provided with half a brain between them."

Old Common smiled.

"Not this time, Norris. Someone's trained them very well."

The fox sighed.

"Ah well," he said solemnly, "we all have our burdens to bear. Did they see you come down here?"

"Yes, they did. I'll have to move out in a minute, before they find the other entrance and block it off."

"Well, you'd better leave right away then. Shall I nip out and give you a hand? Create a diversion and all that?"

"No no," said the hare. "There's no need. I think I can still fix everything." He moved across the chamber to the other tunnel.

"Well, good luck, old boy," said Norris. "When they're gone, drop in for a chat sometime."

"Will you be all right?" said Old Common.

"Oh yes, of course. They won't come down here when they see you leave. And the new fox hunt's not till next week. My word, how tiresome that's going to be! Anyway, you'd better be off."

The hare nodded, turned and went up the tunnel. Norris the fox watched and wished he were a few years younger. The hare was past middle age himself, but he still looked succulent enough. The fox licked his toothless old gums and sighed. Then he put his head between his paws and went back to day-dreaming about woodcocks and snails.

The hare was outside now, hunched at the mouth of the burrow, blinking in the rain. His nose pointed almost straight ahead as he looked nervously to the right. The dogs were snuffling at the toes of a bush, but moving closer all the time. He bit his lip and waited.

He glanced away to the left. There was a wide gap between the bushes. The brook lay beyond it. He looked back—and as he did so, the lurcher caught sight of him. It moved at once, leering as it sprang towards him. But the old hare was still very quick. He bounded out of the hole and kicked away along the grass, through the gap in the bush, and down towards the brook.

The wind was hard in his ears but he heard the snapping snarling of the dogs and he knew they were catching him. Soon one of them was very close. He leapt to one side and kept running. The dogs had to change their stride, but they did it with ease. Then they were gaining on him again. They came in at him from both sides, forcing him to abandon his sidesteps and run straight, cutting down his options.

Then the brook was there. A trundling stream, bordered by sapling willows and high reed-grass, swollen and spottled with rain. Frantic as he was, the hare's brain was still working quite coolly. He decided not to go left, where the bank was high and very steep, but down to the right through the thick grass. The dogs were right on his tail now and his lungs were in pain, but he forced himself through the grass and took off in a last long leap out across the brook.

He hit the water just as the dogs reached the bank behind him. They jumped in after him, but he had a head start—and he was a strong swimmer. The dogs were not. They thrashed about in the water and splashed a lot of it up their noses, but the hare stayed as calm as he could and pulled himself across to the other bank. Before his pursuers could reach him, he was gone through the long grass into the next field.

Now the strain of the chase caught up with Old Common. There was a thin pain in his legs and chest and he knew he couldn't outrun the dogs anymore. He was too old. He had to hide again. A quick dash to the right took him to the edge of the field—and a row of long poplar trees. Under the wet roots of one of these trees, hidden by grass, he found another of his old hideouts, another tunnel. He dived into it and dragged himself through to the narrow central chamber where he collapsed and lay sobbing with the effort. Outside, the two dogs were looking for him again, smelling the grass and prowling along towards the line of poplars. Their work was methodical, unhurried, and utterly tireless. They were drenched to the skin and didn't even think about it.

In the burrow, Old Common heaved the damp air into his body. He was still recovering, very slowly, when he heard a sound, something moving in the chamber beside him. He held his breath to listen, but not for long. His lungs were tight with pain. He tried to breathe quietly. The thing moved again. He could see its eyes in the blackness, but not much else.

"Who are you?" He blurted the words out. The thing didn't answer, but he thought he saw it move. It seemed to be backing away from him.

"This is no time—" he paused for breath—"not the time for playing games. Who are you?"

The thing shifted in the dirt. It came closer and huddled in front of him.

"Please," it said, in a small hesitant voice, "my name's Hopscotch. I'm a hare like yourself. I don't want to be any trouble."

It was a young hare, scrawny and grey. Old Common had almost stopped panting but his head was hot. He wasn't pleased to see the hare.

"What are you doing in here?" he demanded. "This is my burrow."

"Oh, I'm sorry," said the hare. "I didn't know. I heard some dogs barking across the stream and came in here to hide."

Old Common nodded.

"Fair enough," he said. "But we're neither of us very safe as yet. Those dogs will most likely be here any minute."

"Oh no!" cried Hopscotch. "They'll kill us! We've got to get out!"

"All right, all right, take it steady. They haven't found us yet, and if they get here we'll find a way to get past them. We can start off by keeping calm."

"But they'll kill us!" wailed the hare. "I've seen dogs before. They're huge and big teeth and everything. They'll bite us. We've got to get away!"

"Listen," hissed Old Common. "I've been giving dogs the slip for years. So I know what I'm talking about, see? All we have to do is keep our nerves in one piece and wait for them to make a mistake. They always leave you a way out in the end."

The youngster shook his head like something in a trance.

"No!" he squealed. "We can't get out! They'll kill us with their teeth and biting and we can't get away—"

"Shut up!" The old hare stood up on his hind legs, leaned back, and boxed the other's head with his paws, cuffing his cheek and ears till he was quiet.

"That's better," he said grimly. He put his front legs down and lowered his voice. "Now listen to me. I don't want you to say anything, or do anything too sudden. Just follow close behind me and do everything I do. Got that?"

The youngster nodded meekly.

"Good. Now it's time—"

He broke off when he heard a sound from the opening to the burrow. A dog sniffing. It growled, and the noise filled the dark chamber. Hopscotch started a scream but the old hare stifled it with his paw. Outside, the dog was joined by its partner and they snorted and barked down the tunnel. They knew they were in the right place. The smell of fresh hare was unmistakeable.

Old Common didn't move. He didn't want to run anymore. Perhaps he could just stay here out of reach and wait for the dogs to go away. The tunnel was far too small for them and he was prepared to wait all day and night .if necessary.

Then he heard something he'd been half expecting to hear. Something he'd been dreading. A scratching noise. The dogs were digging their way in.

"Quick!" he said. "This way. Do whatever I do—and nothing else."

The young hare followed in silence as Old Common crept along a side-tunnel.

Then they were outside, in the rain. It was more than a drizzle now. The mouth of their escape hatch was obscured by a straggle of wild oats that merged with the bank of grass and weeds running along the edge of the field just in front of the line of poplars. Old Common stuck his nose out of the hole and looked to the left. The dogs were on the right. He could see the greyhound digging in the wet soil. The lurcher was standing to one side, inspecting the grass with its nose and paws, searching for the other entrance to the burrow. Sometimes it would look up and let its eyes roam around, hunting. They were small eyes, green and black, and Old Common couldn't look at them for very long.

Then the lurcher moved away, behind the digging greyhound, round the tree, investigating it from all sides. For a while it was out of sight—and the old hare saw his chance. Without a word he hopped slowly away to the left, behind the line of grass, taking Hopscotch with him. There was no pursuit. The greyhound went on scrabbling in the mud and the lurcher was nowhere to be seen. Old Common looked back for a moment then turned and went on. The corner of the field was getting slowly closer—and with it the sanctuary of the stream. Once they were across that, the dogs would surely never find them.

And then he stopped. He didn't breathe. The lurcher was there in front of them, blocking the way to the brook. There was no way past it.

But the dog wasn't looking in their direction. It had walked in a circle round the tree and then moved off towards the river with no real purpose. It was just looking. Now it strode across the grass and moved back along the edge of the field towards the tree and the greyhound. But it didn't get there. For some reason it stopped, and instead of by-passing the two crouching hares it stood quite still beside them, separated only by that thin rank of weed grass. And there it stayed, standing looking around, ignoring the strong drizzle. Old Common looked up at the vast brindled body shining with rainwater. He knew it was only a question of time before the dog glanced down under its nose—but he also knew there was nothing else he could do but just stay still and hope they weren't seen. The lurcher turned its head. The green-black eyes hardly moved as they searched the ground in front of them. They looked to the right, glanced at the field on the left, then— to Old Common's horror—they gazed down at the line of grass by the great dog's feet.

Even then the lurcher didn't see them—but suddenly the pressure became too much for young Hopscotch. With a short yelp he jumped out from behind the grass wall and dashed out right under the lurcher's nose, screeching with terror.

"No, I can't!" he babbled. "I'm going and gone! I can't anymore!"

He took them all by surprise. Old Common had no time to catch hold of him and the dogs reacted late. But then they were away, barking and storming across the soaking grass towards the hare. Hopscotch was too terrified to think clearly. He jumped left and right through pure habit, but the last of his jumps took him very close to the greyhound. It lifted his cheek and eyeball away from his head and cut short his squealing, with a single bite. The lurcher was there in seconds, but the hare was dead by then. And Old Common watched it all without a sound.

He silently cursed the young hare's lack of nerve, but he wasn't unhappy. It had saved his hide. The dogs had made their kill and they would be satisfied. One hare was as good as another.

But once again he'd misunderstood these hounds. Especially the lurcher. While the greyhound poked at the small remains with its paw, the brindled dog looked up sharply and peered through the rain at the row of poplars. It looked down at the dead hare, then back up. It walked across the grass. The greyhound watched, barked questioningly, then followed it towards the trees.

Old Common scowled as they came closer. For the first time he realised just how much his death meant to these dogs—and to their owner. Could they really hate him so much for eating a few cabbages and carrots over the years? Now, for the first time, he had no plans, no strategy left. He'd tried everything and yet here they were, coming over to end his life. There was nowhere to hide, no time for thinking. The hare did the last thing he wanted to do. He ran out to meet them.

The dogs were surprised but taken aback only for a

second. They growled, yelping, broke into a run. When they were close enough, the hare leaned in towards them, then stopped them in their tracks by sidestepping off his right leg and shooting across the grass towards the stream. The dogs turned and surged after him, gaining, squelching in the slush grass. Old Common pinned back his ears and made a bee-line for the brook. There was no point jumping about from side to side this time. He had to save his strength.

He was very close to the stream now. He could see the rain splintering on it. Soon he'd be in the water and perhaps across to the other side. Then what? He couldn't hide anywhere and the dogs were still strong. He knew he had to avoid the stream to survive.

He'd almost reached it when he suddenly swerved to the right and ran along the edge of the bank. The dogs slowed down, then picked up speed and went after him. There was pain in his legs again, a sharp weight in his chest. He went on running, turning away from the brook altogether. The dogs moved out wide to cut him off, forcing him back towards the water. He ran till the greyhound was nearly upon him, then he stabbed away with a fierce muscular jerk—and flew right between the dogs as they bore down on him. He felt the lurcher's hind leg brush his side as he passed. Again he'd surprised them, buying a little more time, a few paces more. But he was tiring very fast now and the heavy ground seemed to be sucking him into it. As he ran in a straight line towards the gentle bushes on the rim of the stream, he heard the dogs closing in on him from behind. They were barking with excitement now, knowing he couldn't outstrip them. There were only bushes ahead, then the stream. There they would kill him.

The hare didn't bother to look back. He put all his energies into one last mad splash across the grass and into the bushes. He was running full pelt. So were the dogs— and they didn't bother to slow down. The bushes were thin and pliant. There were no thorns on them.

Old Common got there a stride in front of them. He rippled through the bushes and as he came out on the other side he braced himself for one final sidestep. The hedge was almost right on the edge of the bank. There was no slope, just a long unexpected drop to the water below. The hare knew this from the start. The dogs didn't. He jumped away to the left a second before the greyhound came arrowing through the bush.

Its whoop of triumph changed to a yowl of fear and surprise as it saw nothing but the water in front of it. It tried to use its front legs as a brake but the wet ground gave way and the greyhound only succeeded in snapping its left ankle before it fell into the water. Old Common heard its scream of pain as he hustled away along the bank.

The lurcher was right on its partner's heels. It wasn't quite as fast, so it had more time to see what was going on. And its brain worked faster. Instead of trying to stop, it made the best of a bad job by jumping out into the air to avoid landing on the greyhound when it hit the water.

Further along the bank, Old Common had stopped for a quick rest under the nearest bramble bush. He listened to the sounds of the dogs: the snarling and throaty anger of the lurcher, the clipped yelps of the greyhound with the fractured foot. And soon, for the second time that morning, the loud alien curses of the owner of the hounds. After a while the dogs were pulled out, but by then the hare was gone, allowing himself one brief smile before running off across the fields to lose himself in the long grass and the drizzle.

By the time it stopped raining, Old Common was relaxing under a shrub of hawthorn on the crest of a hill, gazing out over the green slopes and nibbling at a brussels sprout. His fur was drying, the sun was coming out. Life was good.

Then he remembered the agonies of the early morning. The pain in his lungs and the fear. He was old now—it was time to face the fact. It wasn't a game any more. Perhaps he would have to move away, end his days in a foreign place, somewhere safer. He chewed the crisp green vegetable and shrugged. After all, he was still here. The dogs had been fast and strong and quick-thinking. They'd been good dogs, in a different class from the rest. And he was still there. He'd beaten them. True, he'd been lucky when the young hare lost its head, but in the end only his own quick wits had saved him. He'd been right to keep his faith in the idea that the dogs would make a vital mistake somewhere along the line.

But perhaps next time there would be even better dogs, better trained, hungrier. Perhaps next time they would kill him. The hare looked at the thinning clouds and the sun, and smiled. Somehow he doubted it!

G O B

A T SUNSET, THE TALL PINE TREES ON
one side of a large forest clearing cast their shadows on the vast spread of bramble that occupied a corner
of the same clearing. Deep inside this tangle of thorns,
something small and nimble was moving.

It was very brown and it moved like a mouse, creeping
and scuttling along the bramble stems, squeezing through
the tiniest gaps. But it wasn't a mouse, it was Nippa the
wren going back to her nest.

She was returning from a short hunting trip and she was
moving very quickly because she hated leaving the nest at
any time, even for food and water. Her eggs were in the
nest, her seven newly laid, very special eggs—her very first
batch. Her big brown husband had left her before they
appeared, but she didn't mind that in the least. Her eggs

were all she wanted—and she had to get back to sit on them.

It was almost dark when she arrived at the nest. It was a small, tight, beautifully woven ball of moss tucked into a gap at the end of a rotting old log lying on its side just inside the bramble patch. The nest was perhaps a little exposed, but there was a fat wedge of nettles in front of it and the log itself was a perfect site. It was strong and thick and the nest was high off the ground, so it was really quite safe.

There was a tiny hole in the moss, and Nippa was about to slip inside it when she saw something through the bank of nettles, something moving across the clearing. The shadow of a bird—but she couldn't tell what kind of bird it was. It was a shadow she'd seen before, while she was building her nest, and she didn't like the look of it. She frowned, looked around, then slid into the nest.

Once inside, her frown disappeared when she saw her eggs. She chirped as she looked at them, and her eyes were very bright. The first thing she did was count them. They were all there, as usual. Seven tiny white eggs, faintly speckled with reddish brown. She fairly squirmed with pleasure as she sat down to keep them warm.

It was only then that she realised that something wasn't quite right. She found she couldn't sit comfortably on the eggs. She got up and looked very hard at them. One was much larger than the others, and the speckles on it were more black than brown. She couldn't understand why she hadn't noticed it before. She narrowed her eyes and poked at it with her foot. Then she decided that it had always been larger and that in her excitement she simply hadn't noticed it. It seemed the only way to explain it. After all, she'd laid seven eggs and there were still seven eggs in front of her. So she shrugged and smiled and settled back on top of them. Perhaps the bigger egg meant she would have an especially large and healthy chick. She closed her eyes, wriggled her upright little tail, and went, very happily, to sleep.

The days passed slowly and warmly in the neat little nest as Nippa sat and waited for her eggs to hatch. Sometimes she had to go out and look for food, but she always returned within a few hours, and she always had a good look round before coming back in. If she saw any suspicious movement or nearby shadow, she would stay well clear of the nest to avoid leading some hungry prowler to her precious eggs.

Two weeks went by and Nippa knew the eggs were nearly ready, so she left the nest to snatch a last quick meal before they hatched. It was a fierce red sunset and the light that stormed through the little hole in the moss made each of the eggs glow pink and warm.

One of them, the unusually large one, started to crack. The shell began to splinter and fall apart, and soon the bird inside was able to struggle out and stumble around the nest. It was an ungainly little creature, pink and blind and naked, and for some time it just lay on the floor and twitched. But after just a few hours it was strong enough to get up and make a little space for itself . . .

It began by rolling the nearest unbroken egg over, then bent down, lifted it up, carried it on its back to the doorway of the nest—and dropped it out. The egg hit the grass at the foot of the log and cracked. Something small and wet moved inside it. The little bird picked up the next egg and heaved that out of the nest as well. It repeated the operation several times and soon the nest was almost empty.

Then it sat down on the soft green floor with its head in the air and its beak wide open, while a thin gurgling noise came from its pink transparent little throat.

It took Nippa a long time to get back from her little raid. A rat had been wandering through the thicket, and it had seen her, so she'd had to lead it away through the brambles before she could work her way back to the nest. She dived into it at once—and couldn't believe her eyes.

For a moment she thought she was in the wrong nest. Her eggs were gone, her beautiful priceless eggs—and all that was left was this big blind infant with a wide-open beak and gawky pink body. As soon as it heard her come in, it started to make louder noises and crawl towards her.

Nippa stepped back and looked outside, down at the ground. But the eggs were gone, already devoured by some passing predator, and the little wren didn't know what to think. Then, all at once, she decided she didn't care what had happened. Something had taken her eggs away, but one of them had managed to survive—and she was grateful for that.

She hopped back into the nest and stroked the little chick's body with her wing. The noises from its gaping mouth were louder and more insistent.

"Yes, little one, I know. It's food you want. Well, mother will bring you some right away."

She skipped out of the nest and went off to look for grubs. Once again her eyes were bright, and her tail quivered high in the air as she trotted away through the briar patch.

———

Within a few weeks the small pink fledgling had become a full-grown cuckoo called Gob. Like all good cuckoos he was quite content to sit back and allow his foster-mother to feed him and look after him till he was ready to fly away for the autumn.

And Nippa herself was quite happy with the arrangement. She didn't know he was a cuckoo. She didn't know that the shadow she'd seen all those weeks before was the shadow of the mother cuckoo spying on her nest as she built it, then flying away after laying that large egg next to the others. Nippa didn't know any of this, and she didn't care. As far as she was concerned, he was her own son and she was only too happy to fill his face with food and generally see to his needs.

But Gob was a strange and very demanding bird. The only things he would eat were his favourite bristled caterpillars, and he would send the little wren on long dangerous expeditions to find them. What made it even worse was that Nippa couldn't eat any of these caterpillars herself (her stomach simply rejected them) and since the cuckoo had to be fed several times a day, she had very little time to feed herself. So she grew thinner and rather weak, but the cuckoo didn't notice. He was too busy enjoying the warm days and getting fat.

In fact, he became so wide and heavy that he simply burst out of the nest, and Nippa had to repair it at regular intervals. Which in turn meant she had to go out and look for building materials, and it wasn't long before most of her time was spent in flying, hunting for grass and moss and caterpillars. And while all this was going on, the cuckoo never left the nest. Not even once, not even to stretch his legs.

"But why not, little one?" said Nippa. "It can't be good for you to stay in this tiny nest all the time."

"Why shouldn't I?" said Gob, in his usual bad-tempered voice. "I like it here. I don't want to go any-where else."

"But soon you'll have to fly around the forest."

"Why?" he snapped. "I don't need to do that. I've got you to fetch my caterpillars for me."

"Yes," she said, "but there are other things in the forest apart from caterpillars, you know."

"Well," he sniffed, "I suppose those little brown ear-wigs aren't bad, but caterpillars are so much juicier."

"Oh, I don't mean that, little one," she said. "I mean there's more to the forest than just food."

"What?" he snorted, leaning away from her. "More than food? Impossible! What else is there?"

"Well," she said pertly, "there's all sorts of beautiful things to see—and little low winds you can glide on—and the flowers—oh, more than I can tell you! Why don't you fly out there with me and I'll show it—"

"No," said Gob, very brusquely. "I can't be bothered. It's all too much trouble. I'll stay here."

"But really, little one—"

"Oh, shut up!" he snapped. "Since you've got nothing better to do, go out and fetch me another caterpillar. I feel a bit peckish."

"Why not come with me?" she began—but the cuckoo hissed and went for her with his beak, so she jumped away from the nest and flew off across the clearing.

As she dodged her way through the banked grass in the next field, Nippa couldn't help feeling unhappy. Not be-cause she was tired and hungry, nor because of the way her adopted son treated her, but because she couldn't persuade him to fly. Or walk. Or leave the nest in any way. She didn't want him to leave, but she was sure it wasn't a good thing for him to just sit there and eat all day. But then what could she do to change his mind? She didn't know. She gave a sad little shrug and went on looking for his caterpillars.

"Ah!" he said, when she returned to the open nest with a pair of green meals in her beak. "They look all right. Come over here and give them to me."

"Well," she panted, "I'm a little bit tired. Couldn't you just reach over and take them from me?"

"What?" he said aghast. "What, all the way over there?"

"Oh well," she sighed, and she took two steps round the rim of the nest, lifted herself into the air and fluttered above him as she dropped the two caterpillars into his great yawning pot-hole of a beak.

"Hm, yes, not bad," he said. "I quite liked those. Go and fetch me a few more."

"Oh dear," she said, "I'm so tired. Couldn't you wait a little while? Just a few minutes?"

"Oh, I see," he sniffed, sticking his beak up in the air. "Well, if it's too much trouble . . ."

"No, no!" she said hurriedly. "I'll go right away." She gave him an affectionate peck on the cheek. "But I have to go such a long way for that kind of caterpillar. What about a few nice worms instead?"

"No."

"Some earwigs, then? You like those."

"No. I want caterpillars. Now go away and get me some!" He lunged at her with his beak again, stabbing her shoulder as she flew away. "And be quick about it!" he called after her. "You were away too long last time."

Nippa soon forgot the pain in her shoulder. She was

more worried about something else. She'd just seen another shadow—and a bird shooting through the air. It was
hiding in a tree now, one of the tall pines in the clearing
near her nest. She was sure it had seen her, whatever it
was—and she took great care not to venture out into the
open while she searched for more caterpillars. She had to
search for quite a while, and during that time she forgot
about the bird and thought about her son instead. It was
hard to know why she was still fond of him. There were
times when she wasn't. He was never kind or gentle or
considerate towards her, but sometimes, just sometimes,
when he was in a good mood, he would sing to himself in
the warm evenings, in a clear melodious voice that made
all her troubles seem worthwhile. She managed a tired
smile as she hunted through the long grass.

On her way back, she stopped at the edge of the clearing. She wanted to waste no time getting across to her nest
because she knew Gob would be impatient for his food—
but she also knew that if she flew openly across the clearing, the bird in the tree would see her, and he might be
dangerous. She looked hard at the branches of the pine,
the caterpillar flopping around in her thin little beak as she
turned her head upwards. She couldn't see anything in the
tree, but she knew that didn't mean much. She thought of
racing across to the nest as fast as she could, but the risk
was too great. Instead she darted through the thin grass
around the border of the clearing, reached the nettles in
front of the old log, had another long look at the pine
tree, then skipped through the nettles onto the nest.

"What took you so long?" yapped the cuckoo. "Trying
to starve me now, are you?"

"Oh no!" she gasped. "It's just that there's—"

"Oh, do stop talking!" he said. "Just give me that caterpillar."

"Yes of course," she said, flapping up to drop it in his mouth, "but please, little one, keep your voice down just a bit—"

"Why?" he said, in an even louder voice. "I don't want to. Why should I?"

"Please," she whispered. "I think there's something in that tree."

"Well, of course there is!" he shouted. "Leaves and branches and things—anyone knows that. What are you staring at now?"

But Nippa didn't answer. Her head was turned away towards the clearing and her eyes, huge with fear, were fixed on the sleek soaring figure that flew up out of the pine tree. She dropped the caterpillar from her beak.

"Look what you've done!" screamed the cuckoo. "My food! My poor little supper! Just look at it!" He pecked Nippa's head with his beak and she moved aside—but she was too frightened to feel the pain.

"Fly away, little one!" she cried, pointing at the sky with her wing. "There's no time to waste!"

"No I shan't!" said Gob—then he looked up and caught sight of the soaring bird as it dipped and sped towards the nest. He didn't know what it was—but Nippa knew only too well. It was a goshawk, the bantam bird of prey, short and neat and quite deadly. She gave a short chirp of alarm and dived into the depths of the bramble bush, fully expecting her son to move when she did. She knew he was too big to get inside the briar patch, but she thought that now, finally, when the only alternative was death, he would fly away as fast as he could.

But he didn't. He tried to. He had enough sense to be terrified of the diving hawk, but he couldn't get away. In all the weeks since he hatched from his egg, he'd never once moved from the nest, so he'd never learned how to fly.

He waggled his wings and jumped in the air, but he couldn't take off. Instead he just fell off the log, rolled on his side, and lay writhing among the nettles. His bright singing voice had no place here. All he could manage was a bundle of strangled squawks, and when he looked up all he could see was brown-breasted death, with reaching talons and its beak half-open in a smile.

The little nest on top of the rotting old log was empty. A big wren stood next to it and frowned as he looked at it. He heard a pattering of feet in the thornbush beside him, and went in to have a look. He found another wren, a female, walking aimlessly through the briar. She looked sad.

"It's me," he said hesitantly.

She just looked at him.

"I've come back."

Still she said nothing.

"Why are you crying?" he asked.

"My son is dead."

He nodded.

"Your son," he mused. "Yes, he was yours, in a way. But not mine."

She frowned at him.

"It's true," he said, and she looked away, deep in thought.

"And now you're back," she murmured.

"Yes. You can have other sons."

He put the side of his beak on her neck and she smiled.

"Small sons," she said. "I only want small sons."

He smiled and stroked her wing with his.

"We'll make them as small as you like," he said.

KEW

THE DAY WAS HOT AND UNHEALTHY. A real dog-day, the air thick with moisture. One edge of the forest lined up against the feet of a few small hills and the hills knelt by the side of a frowning mountain range studded with pine trees. On the grassy side of one of these hills, there was a weasel. It was stretched out happily in the sun, half-asleep and full of food. The remains of a small rabbit lay beside it. The weasel woke up.

It licked its lips in the heat, tasting the sweet blood of the rabbit in its mouth. It smelt the grass and the hot soil, felt the sun on its neck—but it also sensed something else. It looked quickly over its shoulder. Nothing there. It looked down the hill in front of it, and saw no danger. So it rolled its shoulders and prepared to doze off again. Then, as a formality, it glanced upwards—and as it did so, a massive shadow spread itself across the grass on the hillside, covering the weasel completely and blacking out the sun. The weasel sprang to its feet and bared its teeth in defiance, but there was fear in its face. The shadow spread itself wider, there was a sound of huge flustering wings, and the weasel screamed, just once.

Then there was nothing on the side of the hill. No shadow. No weasel. And no half-eaten rabbit in the browning grass.

"No, Kew. For the last time, no. You are not going up there and that is final."

"I'll be all right," said Kew. "I know I will."

"You know nothing of the sort," said her mother. "You've never been up there and you're not ready to go up there now."

"But when will I be ready?"

"I know when. And when the time comes, I'll take you up myself. But not now and not for a long time yet."

"Mother, I want—"

"That's enough!" said her mother, in a very stern voice. "The subject is closed, Kew. When you're ready, we'll go up together. Until then, you'll just have to be patient."

"Patience," muttered Kew to herself. Patience and waiting. It was always the same old story. The night was nearly over and she was settled in her favourite old fir tree on a slope of the lowest hill. She was alone now. Her mother was asleep in another tree and her father had been dead for some time. Kew was watching the distant mountains, as she watched them every day. Somewhere in among those swaggering peaks was the creature she wanted to see more than anything in the world. Neither she nor her mother had ever seen him before, but she knew he was there. The Lord of the Air, looking down

from his mountain fortress. The great Golden Eagle himself.

For a long time now she'd longed to find him, to fly
high beyond the foothills and be with him—but her
mother had forbidden her to go any higher than the nearest hill. The mountains, she said, were no place for a
young sparrowhawk to visit on her own. And Kew was
young, far too young. She would just have to wait. Besides, her mother would often add, no-one she knew had
ever seen or heard the Golden Eagle. He almost certainly
didn't exist.

But he did exist. Kew was sure of that. And all she
wanted was the chance to go up and find him. It didn't
seem such a lot to ask.

They were the thoughts that had been in her head every
day and night. And they were there again as she sat in her
fir tree, gripping a short branch in her claws.

She looked up and saw the first blush of daylight in the
sky. The air was warm. She felt fit and strong and eager.
Before long, she would be old and weak. Have patience,
her mother had said. But this wasn't the time to be patient. This was the dawn, the perfect time for flying, and
Kew had things to do. A brief flurry of wings and she was
in the air, flying away from the fir tree and the hillside,
away from her sleeping mother, her head turned to the
north and the silent waiting mountains.

The mountains had always looked very close. Kew had
often felt she could just reach out a wing and touch them.
But even though she flew towards them all morning, they
never seemed any nearer. So, when the sun was right
overhead, she started to look for somewhere to rest.

She'd just decided upon a small jag of rocks on the side

of the very last hill when she saw something on the hill itself, quite close beside her. It was only there for a second before it vanished, but she knew she'd seen it and she knew what it was. It was a shadow.

She moved warily away from the hill and flew upwards towards the first of the great mountains. As she passed the foot of the cliff, she saw the shadow again, moving along the rock. It was following her—and it wasn't her own.

She tried looking back, but the sun was in her eyes when she turned her head. She dipped her wings and swept down away from the open spaces, making for the wooded slopes of the next mountain. She flew fast, spurred on by fear, but she hadn't flown very far before she heard the sound of huge wings beating the air behind her. She dived again, swerving to her left, then back to the right—but she could still hear the wings. Down past the side of the next mountain she flew, closing in on the trees at the bottom, forcing her muscles to work harder. The shadow appeared again, on the rocks alongside her. It was much larger this time, and it was growing. She felt the draught from the vast pounding wings, and all at once she knew there was no escape. There was nowhere to hide and the trees below her were too far away. So she turned in towards the side of the mountain and landed on a thin ledge. She turned quickly to face her pursuer, but she could see very little. The huge bird blotted out half the sun but she was still dazzled by the other half and all she could see was a great black shape in the blinding light. Then the sun was totally shut out and she looked up boldly at the black shape, her claws feeble but ready, her face strangely calm.

From somewhere on her right, she heard an urgent hissing voice.

"In here, pipsqueak! Move fast!"

She didn't stop to think. Hopping sideways, she scuttled along the ledge. Something gripped her wing and pulled her backwards into a gap in the rock, out of the daylight into utter blackness.

She heard the frantic flapping of wings outside, and a loud coarse screech from her frustrated attacker. Then it was gone and there was no sound at all.

Kew lay very still in the darkness, fighting for breath. Before she'd recovered, the same hissing voice crept out from the shadows.

"Nearly done for there, weren't you, pipsqueak?"

She looked up, breathing heavily, and saw she was in a bleak narrow cave, a mere slit in the flank of the mountain. She looked in the direction of the voice and blinked. As her eyes got used to the darkness she saw the face behind the voice, looming pale and listless from the back of the cave. It was the face of a wild cat.

Kew took all this in very quickly. She nodded at the cat.

"Thank you," she gasped. "The Eagle . . . couldn't get away . . ."

"Aye," said the cat, "he's fast and cunning enough, that one. Hasn't got the better of me yet, mind you."

"Oh!" said Kew in some surprise. "So you know him well?"

"Know him?" said the cat, and she saw him smile. "Why, pipsqueak, I've been outwitting that old white-tail eagle for as long as I can remember."

"White-tail eagle?" said Kew in a weak voice.

"Aye," said the cat. "What did you think it was?" There was a frown on his face. Kew hesitated.

"Nothing," she said unconvincingly. "I was too frightened to think about what it was."

"Hm," said the cat. "Well, that's as may be. But you shouldn't be up here alone, a little bag of feathers like you. There's danger here."

"I know that now," she said wryly.

The cat laughed, in a deep prowl of a voice.

"Well, you're safe enough for now, I suppose. But your place isn't up here. You need to get back down to the woodland where you belong."

"But why?" said Kew. "If the white-tail eagle's gone—"

"He's not the only peril in these hills," said the cat in a slow padded voice. Kew felt her pulse beating faster in anticipation.

"What else is there?" she said eagerly.

"Well," said the cat, almost purring the words out, "there's me . . ."

"Oh!" said Kew, and she took a step backward. Having never seen a wild cat, she'd had no fear of this one. But now that she thought about it, he did look a dangerous customer. She saw his claws, and the edge of his teeth when he talked, and his wiry muscled body.

"But you wouldn't hurt me," she muttered. "I mean— you won't, will you?"

The cat looked hard at her. She saw his shoulder muscles tighten under the fur. Then he laughed.

"Nay, pipsqueak," he chuckled. "Not me. Lost my appetite over the years. And I'm old now. Too bloody feeble to attack anything. Anyway," he sighed, "I won't be around much longer."

"Oh," said Kew hurriedly, "don't say that. You don't look very old."

The cat put a tired smile on his mouth.

"No, not very old, it's true. But I'm finished, pipsqueak. I know it. That's why I stay up here all the time, away from everything. Don't want anyone to see me going."

"But you say you've been up here a long time," said Kew. "How do you survive?"

"Oh, I get by," said the cat. "I still manage to track down a meal or two some nights. But anyway, enough of all this. I'm depressing myself, let alone you."

Kew was about to say something, but the cat spoke first.

"And you, chickpea," it said, "what are you doing up here?"

Kew waited before answering.

"I've always wanted to see the mountains," she said slowly. "So I thought I'd come up and have a look—"

She stopped because she heard the cat growling in the back of his throat. Her eyes opened very wide.

"Don't lie to me, pipsqueak," he said gravely. "No-one comes up to the high rocks just to see the sights. There's too much death here. Tell me the truth."

Kew looked squarely at him and took a quick breath.

"I've come to find the Golden Eagle," she blurted out.

The effect of her words on the cat was immediate. He slunk back to the corner of the cave, hissing through his teeth. The look on his face was terror itself.

"The Eagle?" he spittled. "The Golden Bird? Nay, pipsqueak, that's not what you want!"

"But it is," said Kew brazenly. "All I want to do is see him, just once."

Again the cat hissed.

"Nay!" he said again, shaking his head violently. "No-one sees the Golden Bird. He's death on the wing!"

Kew frowned.

"How do you know?" she demanded.

"I know," snarled the cat. "Believe me, I know. I seen him!"

"You've seen him?" said Kew, and her eyes were bright. "Really? Where? When can I see him too?"

"Never!" cried the cat. "No-one sees the Golden Bird. I tell you, he's death itself. No-one sees him!"

"I don't believe you!" she shouted. "I don't believe he's like that! You say you've seen him and you're still alive. Why should I believe you?"

The cat growled again.

"Why?" he said in a very low voice. "Why should you believe me, little pipsqueak? I'll show you why." And then his voice was suddenly loud and frenzied. "Here's why, curse you! Look for yourself!"

As he said this, the cat turned his back to her—and Kew gasped in horror at what she saw.

There was no fur on the cat's back. Just a patch of wrinkled skin. She could see his bones pushing through it, and there were thick scars across his rib-cage. One of his shoulders was out of place and his left hindleg was missing. All that was left of it was a thin stump.

Kew didn't know what to say. She just went on staring at the cat's mutilated back. He turned round.

"That's the Eagle's work," he said, in a much quieter voice. "Long time ago." He paused. "You can't fight the Golden Bird," he added. "You can only run or fly. I didn't run fast enough."

"I'm sorry," said Kew, but the cat shook his head.

"Nay, fledgling, it's done now. No sense weeping over it. Mind you," he said, with the trace of a sigh, "there's times I do think about it, I must admit. Times I think of what I was, what I might have been. I was a hunter once, you know. A real hunter. Catch anything, I could. Not now, of course."

Then he stopped and said nothing, his wide blue eyes staring into space. When he felt the young sparrowhawk's wing touching his ruined shoulder, he smiled at her.

"Aye, pipsqueak," he said quietly. "Aye, I know. These stories never raise a smile. But it's done now, as I say."

Kew stroked his ear. She thought she heard him start to purr.

"I'm going to keep searching for him," she said.

The cat frowned at her.

"Even now?" he said. "You've seen what he can do."

"I know," she said placidly, "but I can't help it. I still want to see him."

The cat looked at her for a moment. The frown on his face disappeared.

"Well, I can't stop you, fledgling. Go up and find your Golden Eagle. Most likely he'll find you first. But either way he'll be the death of you."

Kew didn't answer. She looked at the cat, then stroked his nose and hopped away to the mouth of the cave. In no time, she was gone, leaving the crippled wild cat to himself. He made an awkward movement, as if to get up—but he couldn't. A spasm of pain passed across his striped features and he lay still, cursing in the darkness.

For a long time, Kew just flew. Always upwards, aiming for the summit of the highest mountain. She couldn't imagine the Lord of the Air living anywhere else. She never stopped flying, even though all her muscles ached for a rest and the thin air made breathing very difficult. The winds were stronger up here, and they blew her about like a feather. But she used them well, gliding on the updraughts to save her strength. As the sun began to dip behind the hills on the horizon, she found herself up a broad ravine between two mountain walls.

It was a grim, forbidding sort of place. Vast cathedrals of rock on either side, stained red by the last rays of the sun. A freezing cold current of air driving her up in circles. And not a soul in sight. At last she reached the top of the ravine and landed on the peak of the highest mountain. And here she collapsed, her chest heaving as she fought for breath, her eyes pink and glassy.

For a while, all she wanted to do was lie there and die in peace, but soon her breathing was back to normal and she felt strong enough to stand up.

She looked down. Everything was below her. Every single thing. She was alone on the highest point of all. The roof of the world. Exhausted though she was, it was still an exciting thought.

"The highest!" she called out, to herself and the world below. "Kew is the highest!"

Her voice echoed away across the mountain strongholds and she looked up. She wasn't the highest. There was something above her, across a narrow gully on the left.

A white crest of rock jutted out over the gully. She couldn't see what was on it, but it was higher than she was so she had to fly over and take a closer look. She fluttered wearily across the air and landed on the jagged crest. And what she saw there made her heart beat faster and her beak fall open like a broken twig.

It was a nest. A rough pile of sticks festooned with coarse grass and something that looked like heather. But what made her gasp was the size of the thing. It looked wide enough for a whole flock of sparrowhawks and was surely too big for any one bird. There was only one bird it could have belonged to.

Then, without knowing why, Kew looked away across the sky. There was nothing there, apart from the hot scarlet sunset and the mountains. But then something moved in the distance. A black speck, a blot on the skyline, moving closer by the second.

Kew saw it but she didn't look at it for very long. She glanced around for somewhere to hide. There was only a pair of small flat rocks, but they would have to do. If she tried to fly away, she was sure the bird would see her. So she skipped over to one of the two boulders and hid behind it. Then she waited.

She couldn't resist looking round the side of the rock, so she saw the flying shape sweeping closer and closer. She saw the giant grasping wings and the deep chest. She watched as the huge brown bird soared in a graceful arc towards the white ledge. It didn't see her as she saw it land, arching its wings and spreading its seething talons.

It was the Eagle. This time there was no mistake. It had the golden brown head and neck, the gigantic wings and body, the vicious curving beak. But above all it had the *look*, the air of a king of the mountains. The little sparrowhawk simply stared at it, unable to move, her heart jumping in her breast.

The Eagle brought its wings in to its body and stood quite still, facing away across its barren kingdom. It didn't move for a while, then it turned and looked round in the direction of the two small boulders behind it.

Kew drew her head back to avoid being seen as the giant bird took a few strutting steps forward. It had seen her, she was sure of it. She wanted to scream, to show herself, to do something. But all she could do was huddle behind the flat rock and hold her breath. She waited and waited and when nothing happened she sneaked her beak round the side of the rock . . .

She was surprised to see the Golden Bird ripping its nest apart. It clearly hadn't seen her at all. It was calmly tearing into the rugged structure with its beak and claws, pulling out the branches one by one, scattering the grass and heather in the lowing wind.

Kew watched as the Eagle flung the nest over the side of the mountain, piece by piece, then stood and looked around at its handiwork. Satisfied that it was now completely alone, it moved to the edge of the precipice and looked down. Then up at the sky and the dusty pink clouds. It ruffled its feathers.

With its neck extended and its beak half-open, it let out a long screeching cry that shattered through the mountains. A single harsh note. Then nothing. The wind crashed across the ledge and Kew found it hard to keep her eyes open. The sun had slipped further down, turning the sky blood-red and black. And the Golden Emperor just stood there like a statue in the wind.

From where she was hiding, Kew could just see its face, proud and majestic, cruel as its own beak. The shape of the eyebrows gave it a permanently angry look and Kew could find no softness in its features. It sank down and squatted on the rim of the ledge, looking for all the world like some fierce roosting woodpigeon.

Something was wrong. Kew could sense it. But before she had time to really think about it, the Eagle turned its head and looked at her, one enormous eye glaring at her from the side of its head.

Kew's whole body was transfixed. Frozen motionless. All she could do was stare back up into that fearsome eye and wait for the Eagle to strike.

The huge hooked beak opened a fraction, but the Golden Bird didn't speak. For a brief moment there was murder in its eye. Then something like sadness. Then it turned away. She saw its eyelid slide down and heard a strange crackling noise trickle from its throat. The great head slumped forward, the massive body twitched once or twice, and that was all. The Golden Eagle, the dread monarch of the skies, was dead.

It was all so sudden and unexpected that Kew wasn't sure what had happened. Even when she finally found the courage to leave her hiding-place and fly over to the Eagle's body, she couldn't believe he was really dead. She half expected him to open his eyes at any moment. Even in death, the huge creature looked very much alive. She could almost see his muscles rippling as the feathers flirted in the wind.

But she knew he was dead, really dead—even though she didn't want to know. And the shock was all the greater because she'd never thought of him as something that could die. Now she didn't know whether to feel just unhappy or somehow cheated. But it wasn't something she wanted to go on thinking about, so she left.

Just before she flew away, she fluttered up to the Eagle's head and with one firm tug plucked a single tawny feather from the nape of his neck. Then she flew off down the mountain and left the Golden Bird alone on his isolated crag while the wind played irreverently with his great brown gargoyle of a corpse.

———

Kew knew where she wanted to go, and the return journey was easier. By nightfall she'd arrived back at the split in the mountain where the old wild cat lived.

She put the golden feather on the ledge outside the cave, then edged backwards into the den, pulling the feather in behind her. She turned round and saw the cat lying peacefully in the corner with his eyes shut and his head resting on his shoulder. She dropped the feather on the floor.

"Hello," she whispered, hoping to wake him gently. "I've brought you something."

When he didn't answer, she hopped up to him with the feather in her beak.

"Wake up," she said. "Don't you want to see what I've brought you?"

She bent down and tickled the cat's nose with the feather. He didn't move. So she put the feather down and shook him by the shoulder. But the cat didn't wake up. His head fell a little to one side and lolled about on his chest, but that was all.

"Oh no," murmured Kew. "No, not you too."

She didn't know what to do now, or what to feel. She laid the useless feather between the wild cat's paws and touched his face with her wing. She thought she saw his face brighten just for a moment, but it was probably a trick of the bad light. She turned and hopped out of the cave.

Outside, the wind had dropped and the early night was dry and nondescript. Kew shuffled her wings before flying away. She went to look for food and water, and neither her mother nor anyone else ever saw her again.

MUGGER

T WAS MORE AUTUMN THAN SUMMER
now, and the sun had no great heat in it. The first
dead leaves began floating down to the banks of the great
river and were trampled underfoot. In some places they
had a long way to fall, drifting down from the windswept
heights of grey birch trees—but along the last slow bend
of the river it was a different matter.

Here the branches were so low and heavy they brushed
the mud, and the riverbank itself was almost hidden by
yellow curtains of willow and laburnum and purple
cuckooflowers, all drinking in the wet riches of the river
and the gentle sun.

There was a gap in all this teeming foliage, a slope of
mud between a green beech tree and one of the many
willows. It was a well-trodden slope, a natural drinking
path, and there was something lodged in the mud at the

foot of it. Something thick and brown-red, bloated with riverwater and vivid in the sun. It was half-chewed and bulbous, and in those surroundings it should have been out of place, an obscene thing—but it wasn't. It was beautiful. The sunlit body of a red deer.

Dead, of course. Long dead and waterlogged. Some of it had been pulled away. The hind legs, the rump, and half the ribs—they were all gone. The neck had been broken, so the thin regal head was turned at a ridiculous angle, the antlers on one side trenched in the mud, the other side high in the air. The stag's mouth was closed, its eyes wide open, and there was a dull peaceful look on its face.

The corpse was not alone. There was a small group of animals watching over it. An old squirrel, two rabbits, a heron, and a skinny badger with one of its legs missing. They were standing, saying nothing, in the thick grass at the top of the slope, looking down at the deer. And they were sad. More than sad, for this wasn't the body of just any old stag. It was the lord of the forest, Arcan himself.

For a while the animals just stood around looking miserable. The badger frowned and wiped his whiskers. One of the rabbits hid her face in the other's fur. And the heron stared down at its feet.

"I did not wish to live and see this day," it said, and the badger nodded.

"I still can't believe it," he muttered. "I didn't think Arcan knew how to die."

The smaller rabbit looked up from her cousin's shoulder.

"Perhaps it isn't Arcan," she said in a faint voice. The others didn't answer. They gave her a few blank looks, then turned away. It was Arcan all right. There could be no doubt about that.

The old squirrel had a frown on his face. It made him look almost as ugly as his nephew, the hideous Reek.

"What I can't understand," he grumbled, "is who killed him. I just can't work it out."

"Does it matter?" sighed the heron. "Surely the brutal fact that he is dead is bad enough."

"Yes," said a rabbit, "we should be mourning the Great Lord, not worrying about who killed him."

The old squirrel made a face.

"Well, I don't know about that," he said. "Great Lord or not, there's no point crying over spilt blood. The fact is, anyone who'd dare to kill the old stag has no respect for the ways of the forest. He—or she—could be very dangerous."

"That's a good point," grunted the badger.

"Yes indeed," said the heron, gazing solemnly down its beak at the squirrel. "A very good point. Whoever did this unholy thing is no friend of the forest. But perhaps 'dangerous' is as yet too strong a word."

"I don't see why," retorted the squirrel. "If it could kill Arcan, it must be something very big."

"It wasn't a badger," said the badger.

"No-one said it was."

"A badger wouldn't do such a thing."

"To be sure, friend, to be sure," said the calm heron. "We are all in agreement with you. But let us probe a little further into this tragedy. The good squirrel is of the opinion that the assassin must be a creature of some considerable size. Let him now tell us why he believes this to be so."

The squirrel, sitting on his haunches, pointed impatiently with his finger.

"Well, just look at him," he said. "His legs and half his

body have been pulled away. It takes more than a mouse to do that. And what about those two bite-marks on his side? Whoever made those must have a pretty good set of teeth."

"Well, it wasn't a badger," huffed the badger, after licking his own hefty fangs. The others ignored him.

"Yes, you may indeed be right," said the heron, nodding its head. "Perhaps we should go down and take a closer look at our Great Lord—in the future interest of the forest."

They all agreed, even though the rabbits were none too keen on the idea. They were both a little squeamish.

So they went down the slope and stood close to the soaking body, the four mammals crouching in the mud and the heron standing high on its legs like a bag on stilts. Even when it bent down to examine the corpse, it was still taller than the others.

"This is indeed a grievous thing to behold," it announced. One of the rabbits started to cry.

"Well," said the old squirrel, clearing his throat in a businesslike manner, "I still think it was something big that did it. A large dog fox, perhaps."

The badger shook his head.

"Very few foxes round here," he said, "unless you count old Norris—and he couldn't bite his way out of a broken cobweb. Anyway, I don't know any foxes who'd do something like this."

"What about the rats?" asked the larger rabbit. "There are always plenty of those along the river."

"That's true enough," said the badger, but the heron shook its head.

"Not so, friend," it said gravely. "They have all but vanished. It is said that their king is no longer alive."

"Oh, I hope so!" said the rabbit.

"Anyway, that doesn't concern us," said the old squirrel. "Rats are too small. None of them could have left a set of teeth-marks like that. It must have been something much larger, I'm sure of it."

The badger and the rabbits nodded as they stared at the dead deer. The heron, however, sank its head into its shoulders and cleared its throat.

"Friends," it proclaimed, "the honourable squirrel has formed and expressed his theory on this matter—and a very fine and tenable theory it is too. Now, friends—" it gave a quick light cough—"allow me to expound a theory of my own."

The badger and the squirrel groaned, but the heron took no notice.

"We are beside a river, friends—and rivers are made of water. Water, as we know, is something we drink; and it is something that drowns. It can drown anything, anything that breathes. Even a royal stag. Is that not so, friend squirrel?"

"Yes, yes," said the squirrel, with an impatient wave of his paw.

"Well then," declared the heron, with an air of triumph, "there we have it, the reason for the death of the forest lord. He has come to the river to drink, he slips in the mud, and (being no longer a zestful young buck) he is swept away by the fierce summer current which drowns him at its pleasure. After which, his majestic body, its sinews loosened by the water, is gnawed and eaten, not by one large predator but my many small sets of teeth. And so he comes to rest where we have found him. Dead and despoiled, certainly—but scarcely murdered."

And the heron finally stopped talking. There was a

short silence and the badger shrugged. He, like the rabbits, was convinced the tall bird was right.

"That's all very well," said the squirrel, "but it doesn't explain those large bite-marks."

"It seems to me," answered the heron, "that we have made the mistake of believing that because those marks seem large to us now they must always have been so. However, if we look closely at the remainder of the body, we see that it has been gorged by the water and so appears larger than it was before the drowning. As the body has filled with water and increased in size, so too have those marks. In reality, they are but the tracks of small teeth swollen to a deceptive size."

After this, the heron felt it had said enough for the time being, so it finished talking and stood quietly in the mud with its eyes shut and its long beak in the air. The picture of serene self-importance.

"Yes," said the old squirrel. "Well, you could be right, I suppose. Mind you, I find it hard to imagine anyone taking a bite out of old Arcan's body, even if he was dead."

"What about that huge great stoat?" said the badger.

"Oh, he's dead, he is," said the smaller rabbit, whose name was Bellhop. "He fought the big pike and they killed each other in the water. Or so they say."

"Ah," said the squirrel. "Well, that doesn't leave any-one else I can think of."

"On the contrary," said the heron. "It leaves us with almost anybody and everybody. After all, the great stag, once dead, was no longer lord of the forest. To those who search the river for their meals, he must have appeared as just another food-parcel."

The old uncle pursed his lips.

"I can't argue with that," he admitted.

And nor, as it happened, could any of the others. So they left it at that and walked back up the slope before going off to spread the sad news. The old squirrel was still not convinced about Arcan's killer, but he had no alternatives to offer so he said nothing. The heron, of course, was certain it knew what had happened. The badger, hobbling away on his last three legs, was perhaps not quite so sure —but one thing he did know: whoever had killed or bitten or half-eaten the great stag could not have been a badger!

Vim the vole didn't know the lord of the forest was dead. He was swimming up the river, thinking happy thoughts. He was an old vole by now, rather slow and fat, and his eyesight wasn't very good. But it didn't worry him. His life had been a long one, long and very full. He was content.

Before the river reached the forest it moved through wide acres of meadow and ploughland, very thick with grass and mud. There were a few hedges here and there, the occasional willow tree sinking its roots in the water, but otherwise there was nothing to disturb the bleak flatness of the fields. It was a monotonous, almost desolate place, almost a marsh—but Vim liked it. After the hustle and bustle of the forest, he found it very peaceful and relaxing. There was nothing he liked better than to paddle along this stretch of water and think his own thoughts.

Today he was thinking about two things in particular. His lifetime of good luck, and his loud wife.

He'd always been very lucky, in everything he did—and everybody knew it. No-one could understand why, but Vim didn't even try to understand. To him it was just one of those things, and he was very grateful for it. After all, without his luck he would never have survived. He re-

membered how Na the stoat had saved him from the giant
pike, and how the pike had saved him from Na. Then,
when he was taken by the rats, they'd let him live long
enough for the huge toad to come and rescue him. And
the great Arcan, no less, had sent him home before the
toad himself could feed on him. Yes, he had to admit that
life had often stepped aside to let him pass. He had no
complaints.

He peered at the riverbank as he swam. The sun was
covered by cloud now, and with his short sight he found it
harder to see exactly what was going on. But everything
was very quiet and still. No noise, no sudden movement.
Just the distant zigzag of a snipe or two. It was a good
solid day for a swim.

The vole turned his thoughts to his wife, his big blustery
female. She had no name of her own, so he'd christened
her Mayhem—and it suited her down to the ground, large
bullying creature that she was. She rarely gave him a
moment's peace and the echoes of her endless nagging
filled his head even while he slept. He sometimes wondered if she was the price he had to pay for all his good
fortune, and at times he couldn't help thinking he'd been
given the rough end of the bargain!

But for all her faults he was still very fond of her. At
least there was no chance of her quietly boring him to
death! And she had, after all, presented him with a whole
regiment of sons and daughters, all of them as loud as
their mother and all of them quite perfect. No, he decided
—as he always did—there was nothing in his life he could
ever want to change.

Still, it was good to get away from the family burrow
from time to time. He kicked his legs out a little harder,
swam a little faster, just for the sake of it. He looked to

the left, saw he was passing one of his old favourite willow trees, and swam across the current towards it.

He knew every branch on this tree. He would have recognised it in any weather, even with his weak eyesight. It was a peculiar old thing, a thick meshwork of branches, like hard arteries twisting down into the earth. The main trunk had split in half under the soil, a good clean splice —and the weight of the branches had pulled each half away from the other, so that the whole thing looked like two very close but separate trees, each with a dozen heavy roots showing through the mud and piping into the water.

As Vim started to drift past the willow he noticed that one of its roots looked rather longer and larger than the rest. Thicker and less knotted. He didn't remember having seen it before. He squinted at it and swam a little closer. It really was a strange sort of root, very wide and flat, lying almost straight along the surface of the water. Whereas the rest of the tree was pale brown and almost white in places, this was a darker thing altogether, grey-green in colour. As Vim came right up next to it, he detected a ridge of crusts along the side of it—and two small holes at the very tip, very close to him.

He started to drag himself out of the water onto the root—and then it moved. It rolled suddenly to one side, split open at the end, and showed itself to be not a root but the huge and hideous body of a fully grown croco-dile.

The long twisting jaws opened—and crashed shut. The water swilled and swaggered for a moment—then the great reptile slithered into the river and nosed its way downstream, enjoying its light tasty snack.

Luck had finally run out for Vim the vole.

———

There could be no doubt now about the way Arcan the stag had met his death—and before long everyone in the forest knew it. The huge crocodile made quite a difference to their way of life.

It began by digging itself a series of wide tunnels in the riverbank, some of them hidden by roots, others in the squelching reed-beds. Then it would simply wait, sometimes for hours on end, dipping into its endless supply of patience, waiting for someone to come dawdling up the river. A duck, perhaps, or a water vole, a fox—anything that came to the water to eat or drink. The crocodile was equipped to kill them all. It snapped up the smaller creatures with one movement of its jaws, knocked the dogs and fallow deer into the river with a blow of its tail and dragged them underwater to drown. Anything it couldn't eat at one sitting was heaved away to one of its riverside chambers or pulled down into the river itself and wedged under an old stone or tangle of roots. There the body would lie and soak till the reptile was ready. Then it would grasp a mouthful of wet bloodless flesh and wrench it away from the carcass by spinning along the axis of its long body, like some green underwater dancer plucking the stuffing out of an old velvet armchair.

Before the week was out, everyone had learned to stay well clear of the river for as long as they could, but the crocodile didn't go hungry. It was quite happy to drape itself round the base of a tree in the very heart of the forest, looking for all the world like just another moss-backed log—and wait, for rats and badgers and squirrels. At other times it lay sunning itself in fields of long grass, or in a ditch, or under a hedge. There was no escape from it, no part of the forest it couldn't reach. Only the tree-dwellers and birds could feel safe anywhere, and then only if they stayed well above the ground. The mice and moles and other burrowers spent their days in hiding and their nights in quick and fearful hunting trips. The river was soon deserted and the fields left in the hands of the rooks and crows, for no-one could be sure where the monster reptile would turn up next. Every shadow, every rustle in the bracken became a threat, a hostile thing.

Soon a dreadful stillness and quiet came down on the great forest, a silence filled with heartbeats and fear. Something had to be done about it—and fast. But what? Nobody seemed to know.

"Well, I still say we should get out while we can," muttered the big fat frog. It was squatting with the rest of them on a grassbank just outside the forest at first light. Reek's uncle was there, and Reek himself, with the crippled badger, Bellhop the rabbit, and the frog. The tall heron was there too, but it was keeping very quiet, standing a few paces away from the others as it stared at the ground and looked glum. Everyone else was talking in loud whispers.

"If we stay here, we'll all end up in that monster's belly," the frog was saying. "It's only a matter of time. We've got to get out—and soon."

"What, and leave the forest?" frowned the badger, and the two squirrels shook their heads.

"There's no other choice," hissed the frog. "We can't go on living like this, like a bunch of criminals."

"I know," said the badger. "But the forest—"

"Yes, yes, the forest!" snapped the frog. "There's no need to go on repeating yourself. Can't you understand? We've all got to get out. We can't survive here much longer."

"But I was born here," mumbled the badger. "We all were."

"Yes, and we'll all die here too, the way things are going. Our only chance is to get away."

"No," said Reek's uncle, very firmly. "The badger is quite right. The forest is our home, the only world we know. There's no question of anybody leaving it. After all, frog, where else can we go?"

The frog opened its mouth, closed it, and frowned.

"Well," it mumbled, "if anyone's got a better idea . . ." and it shrugged.

"Somehow," said Reek, "don't ask me how, but somehow we've got to fight this lizard, find a way of destroying it."

"Yes," said his uncle, "or send it back to where it came from."

"Wherever that might be," said the badger.

"Oh, who cares where it came from?" snorted the frog. "And what's all this nonsense about fighting? Who's going to fight it—and with what? There's no-one who can face up to that thing, and we all know it."

Bellhop the rabbit lifted her ears a fraction.

"Isn't there anyone who can help us?" she said quietly. "There always has been up to now."

"Yes," scoffed the frog, "up to now there's always been a big hero somewhere. Arcan, for instance!"

Reek ignored the frog.

"What about Arcan's son?" he asked his uncle. The old squirrel shook his head.

"No, ugly one. The boy's too young, still only a calf. He doesn't know enough to help us."

"What about the toad then?" said the badger. "Is he strong enough?"

The old uncle sucked in his cheeks and wiped something from his whiskers.

"He might be—if he were here. But no-one's seen Ug for weeks now. And besides, I think we'll need more than brute strength to sort this out."

The fat frog broke into a jeer and the sudden noise startled the others.

"Keep your voice down, you!" snarled the badger. "If the lizard hears you we're finished."

"Never mind all that," said the frog. "Now listen to me, all of you. Every one of our great heroes is either dead or gone away. Arcan, Ug, even the big eagle (if he ever existed at all). The old stag's son is useless and the biggest badgers have all been killed by the monster."

"It wasn't their fault," murmured the badger. "At least they stood their ground. They didn't try to save their skins by running away. They stayed to fight the lizard."

"Yes," sneered the frog, "and a fat lot of good it did them, the idiots!"

The badger snarled and his eyes went white with rage, but the old squirrel put a paw on his shoulder to calm him down. The frog jumped away a pace and kept half an eye on the badger as it spoke.

"Let's face it," said the frog, "there's no-one left to help us. We're on our own now. We can't fight this beast and we can't go on hiding and creeping about in the shadows for ever. But at least we're still alive. We can still get out of this place—and persuade everyone else to come with us. Maybe we can come back if the lizard starves to death while we're away—but first we've got to leave. It's the only chance we've got left."

It stopped talking and looked around at the others, defying them to disagree with it. They didn't. In the silence, the old squirrel looked round to the left.

"Hey, lofty," he said, "haven't you got anything to say about all this?"

The heron lifted its head very slowly. It looked mournfully at them for a moment, then stared back at the ground, shaking its head.

"No, friends," it sighed. "I was so sure I knew the cause of the lord Arcan's death. I was wrong. My opinions are of no worth anymore."

The others didn't know what to say to that, but Reek's uncle hopped across the grass and stood in front of the long bird, looking up into its face.

"Now look here, lofty," he said sternly. "You can't go on like this. So you made a mistake. Well, we've all done that before. Besides, no-one else knew who killed the old stag any more than you did. And it's not as if you killed him yourself, is it? You've done nothing to be ashamed of, so you can stop feeling sorry for yourself and tell us what you think we should do. When you're good and ready, that is."

The heron lifted its head and stared down at the squirrel. Then it took a deep breath, looked around at the others with its wide watery eyes, and started to think.

"Why are we wasting time with all this?" grumbled the frog—but the badger growled, just once, and the frog shut its mouth.

"Friends," said the heron at last, "there is one person I think we can turn to—but I fear you will not thank me for telling you who that person is."

"Why's that?" said the badger.

"Just tell us who it is," said Reek firmly. And the heron breathed another long sigh.

"Malgotha," it said softly—and the name made the others catch their breath. The young rabbit's eyes opened wide with fear and the badger stood up high on his three legs, the fur stiffening along his back. For once, the frog had nothing to say.

"Malgotha, eh?" said the old uncle, sucking his cheeks. "That's a drastic thought if I ever heard one."

"It is, after all, only a thought," said the heron.

"But please," whimpered the rabbit, "this Malgotha—I mean, isn't she just as bad as the big lizard? Some say she's even more terrible. Won't it make things worse if we call her up?"

"That's what I think too," said the badger.

The old squirrel nodded.

"Yes, perhaps it's not a good idea," he said. "But then perhaps she really can help—who knows? We can't be sure what will happen."

"Yes, we can."

They all turned and looked at the frog.

"We can be sure of one thing," it went on. "If we go looking for Malgotha, we're looking for trouble. More likely than not, she'll kill us as soon as look at us. But when all's said and done we've got no other choice. Since no-one seems to want to leave the forest, Malgotha's our only hope. If she can get rid of that brute, all well and good. If not—well, being killed by her seems no worse than taking a trip down the lizard's gullet. We might as well get it over and done with. By all means call her up."

The old squirrel smiled.

"Good," he said grimly. "That seems to be settled. Now all we need is someone to actually go and see the old witch."

"I'm not going," said the frog at once. "If I'm going to die, I'd rather do it here, thanks. I won't go out of my way to kill myself, not even for the forest."

"That's right," snorted the badger, "think of yourself all the time. Damn it, I'll go! It takes more than an old ratbag to frighten us badgers!"

"Malgotha is not a thing to be taken lightly, friend," said the heron.

"I don't care," huffed the badger. "I'll sort her out, don't you worry. Shall I set off now or after dark?"

"Neither," said Reek softly. "You must stay at home, old friend."

"Why?" pouted the badger, standing proudly on his three legs. Reek looked him full in the face.

"Because you're too big," he lied. "The lizard might see you, and that would ruin everything."

"Ah," nodded the badger. "That's true enough. I'll leave it to someone else then."

"What about you, lofty?" said the old squirrel—but the heron shook its head.

"I wish I could," it muttered. "I wish I had the cour-age."

"I don't think any of us is too keen on meeting Madame Malgotha," said Reek wryly, and the rabbit shook her head.

"Well," said his uncle, "it looks like we'll have to find someone else to go—and quickly."

"Good idea, old bones! A perfect idea—just what I was thinking myself!"

It was a new voice, a sudden sound from the under-growth. The badger took a step back and showed his teeth. The frog jumped in the air, and the rabbit ran to hide behind the badger.

"No need to be frightened, playmates!" said the voice. "Anyone would think I was a big lizard or something!"

A quick scuffle in the undergrowth and out jumped the last thing any of them expected to see. A big white mouse, grinning from ear to ear.

"Oh, it's you," said the frog, with distaste. "I might have known."

The mouse gave a brisk little bow with his head.

"The noble and valiant Cheesewire at your service!" he chimed. "Sorry if I startled you."

"Well, what do you want?" growled the badger.

"Me?" said the mouse. "I've come to do you all a favour, I have. I overheard you saying you wanted someone to go and have a word with old mother Malgotha—so here I am."

"You mean you're willing to go?" said Reek.

"Willing and very able, mister ugly. I'll go right away if you want me to."

The others looked at one another and frowned or shrugged.

"Tell me, Master Cheesewire," said the old squirrel, "why are you so keen to do this thing? You must know how dangerous it all is."

The mouse laughed.

"Dangerous, yes," he said. "But exciting too. I could do with some excitement, old bones. There's not a lot of it about just now. Our friendly local lizard hasn't done much to liven the place up, has he?"

"Is that the only reason?"

The mouse grinned at him. "Do you need another one, bones?"

"What is all this?" cried the frog. "Here we are trying

to deal with a deadly serious matter—and along comes the great good-for-nothing of the forest, talking irresponsible rubbish as he always does. We haven't got time to waste on cross-talk and giggling. Let's find ourselves someone we can trust to go and see the old hag."

The badger and rabbit muttered in agreement. The white mouse raised an eyebrow.

"Very good, fat one," he said. "A pretty little speech. But tell me this—if I don't go and see old Malgotha, who will? And how many others will the lizard have killed by the time you find someone else?"

There was no answer. The frog shrugged its shoulders and looked the other way.

"Right then," said Cheesewire, "let's get on with it. Someone had better start by telling me where I can find the old witch."

The heron pointed with its wing.

"You must go far upstream," it said. "Beyond the Lonely Trees. Where the river rises from under the foot of the low hills—there you will find the lair of Malgotha."

The mouse nodded and turned to go.

"See you soon, playmates. I'll bring you the lizard's head on a stick!"

And he was gone, scampering away under the skirts of the forest. The others wasted no time in doing the same, going their own separate ways in the creeping daylight, each of them moving quickly and fearfully through the bushes and wondering if they'd done the right thing in entrusting the safety of the entire forest to a wastrel like Cheesewire.

All through the morning, a small white figure could be seen hurrying along the riverbank, heading upstream.

From time to time it would stop, sit up, watch and listen, then dart off again through the grass and weeds.

It was Cheesewire, of course. The forest freak. Everything a wood mouse shouldn't be. He was far too big, for a start. And he was the wrong colour. His tail was too short and he slept only at night. He was also brash and boisterous instead of quiet and timid, he lived in a tree not in the hedgerows, and the only things he had in common with normal wood mice were a pair of very long ears and a passion for strawberries. In every other way he was completely different. He was also the only mouse in the world with a squint.

As a result of all this, everyone in the forest treated him with a kind of amused intolerance. No-one actually disliked him, but there again he wasn't exactly welcomed with open arms. Nevertheless he was widely regarded with a sort of grudging respect. After all, he was one of the great survivors. All the other so-called wood mice lived in fields, but Cheesewire preferred the forest—and he'd learned, very quickly, how to stay alive in it. Even the handicap of being white and very visible in that dark place didn't bother him. In fact he seemed to thrive on it. It made things more difficult, more dangerous, and therefore more exciting. Which was very important to a mouse like Cheesewire. He was easily bored.

It was late afternoon when the white mouse reached the place where Vim the vole had been swallowed. The heron called it the land of the Lonely Trees. As he ran along the bank he kept an eye on the far side of the river. The soil there spent most of its time falling into the water and the roots of the lonely willows were exposed, forming shadows and small caves in the riverbank. It looked just the place to find a crocodile enjoying its creature comforts.

Cheesewire hadn't seen the big reptile yet, not on this trip—so he was still very wary. He wasn't afraid, but he knew that if he was careless enough to get himself eaten he would never reach the old dark witch—and that was a meeting he didn't want to miss for anything.

He hurried on through this marshy waste, on to where the river was just a stream, clean and twisting, carving its way through an area of hard soil covered with stiff grass and small gorse bushes. In the distance he could see a line of hills, not too far away. The haunts of Malgotha.

Then something came out from behind the nearest bale of gorse.

"Hold still, my lad," it said. "I want you for my supper."

Cheesewire turned and found himself face to face with the biggest brown rat he had ever seen. He guessed at once who it was. The king rat himself, out for a stroll.

"Um . . . listen, Your Majesty," stammered the mouse, "don't get in my way. I'm on a very important mission. I'm going to see Malgotha."

The giant rat grunted.

"Yes," he sniffed, "and I'm flying to the moon tomorrow. I know you too well, snippet. You're a sly one. But now it's time for my supper."

"Look," said Cheesewire, holding his ground. "Malgotha is the only one who can help us get rid of the lizard. If you let me go, you'll miss your supper—but if you eat me, it could be your last meal for a long time. If Malgotha kills the lizard, everything will be back to normal and you can go on eating as often as you like."

The brown king hesitated, but only for a moment.

"No," he said, "I don't trust the old witch. If I don't eat you, she will. And, as you say, food's very scarce. I can't afford to let you go."

And he took a step forward.

"Oh well," said the mouse, with a shrug, "I suppose you'd better eat me then. A meal's a meal, after all—even if it means picking up a little deformity."

The rat frowned.

"What are you talking about?"

"Well, can't you see? My squint of course."

The king examined it with suspicion.

"Had it since I was very young," said Cheesewire, "makes it hard to see. Still, you won't mind when you get used to it."

The rat stepped back a couple of paces.

"And it's catching, you say?"

"Well of course," said the mouse. "My old aunt had it, you know. Got herself eaten by a buzzard one day—and the buzzard caught the squint. Crashed into a tree and killed itself, it did. Horrible way to go. Still, as you say, food's not easy to find nowadays. You'd better eat me while you can."

The king moved further away.

"Oh, come on, your kingship! Have a mouthful or two at least. I can offer you a nice bit of rump or some very tasty spare ribs. A rat's got to eat, after all."

The monster rat snarled at him, showing a set of teeth like giant thorns. He wasn't really convinced by the mouse's tale and Cheesewire knew it. But at least he'd made him hesitate and stand back a little—and that was enough. With one quick sprint he was off and running past the rat, away towards the hills. The huge king made a half-hearted move to chase him, but he was built for strength not speed, and the white mouse had always been very quick. In no time at all he was out of reach, and the rat was left to spit disgustedly on the ground. This really was the last straw. First the big toad had snatched Arcan's son, then the huge lizard had driven all the rats out of their riverside holes, and now he'd been outwitted by a child, a little runt with crooked eyeballs. It was all too much. He clenched his teeth then crawled back into the gorse without a word.

Although the hills had looked very close, it took Cheesewire a long time to reach them. He was tired now, so he stopped for a quick rest and a scratch. The river was now no more than a thin dribble behind a patchwork of boulders and bushes under the foot of the first hill. It was a cold clean place, with only the occasional cries of a wild duck to disturb the crisp silence. There was certainly nothing sinister about it.

The mouse got up to have a look around, moving quickly but very quietly, his eyes wide and restless. He found nothing at all along the river itself, but when he looked up at the hillside he saw a very small opening, just a thin black gap in the rock. It was the place he was looking for.

"Well, Cheesy boy," he muttered, "this is where the fun starts!"

For the first time, he had a couple of second thoughts. After all, it wasn't as if he was paying a visit to his grandmother. He thought seriously of backing away from the whole thing, then he shrugged, blinked, and went up the hill with a grin on his face.

He slipped into the small crevice and found himself in a narrow tunnel that slanted diagonally to the left. It was a long tunnel and he moved along it quite slowly to let his eyes get used to the darkness. At the other end he came across a single room with a low ceiling and he looked inside.

It was very dark in the room, unnaturally dark. The mouse couldn't see a thing, not even the wall beside him. And it stank. The stench of old walls stained for years in piss, and the soft animal smell of dead things. The mouse wrinkled his nose. He looked around the room, his eyes standing out like grapes as he tried to see if there was anything in it.

And then a voice came out of that black room, a thin creeping whisper that made Cheesewire's fur stand on end all over his body.

"You've stopped breathing, little filth," said the voice. "Don't tell me even the game-cock of the forest can't hide his terror in the dark room of Malgotha."

This was followed by a hoarse dry chuckle, then silence. The mouse stared hard at the darkness, but he still couldn't see anything.

"You have my permission to breathe, Master Cheesewire," said the voice. "Or is your fear too great?"

The mouse tried very hard to stop himself shaking, but couldn't quite do it. His mouth was dry and he had to lick his lips before he could speak.

"It's not fear, old mother," he said. "I'm holding my breath because of the smell in here. You really ought to get this place cleaned out once in a while."

"Ah!" hissed the voice. "So there's still some life left in the little sprat! A touch of bravado yet! Well, master mouse, your impudence shall reap a rare crop. Look hard and see, as few have seen before you, the blinding majesty of Malgotha!"

Even as she spoke, the room became less dark. The blackness changed to dark grey, then pale grey, and finally as bright as the clearest dawn. Now the mouse could see that the room was littered with old broken bones and bits of fur. And in the middle of the room, staring at the mouse with her small white eyes, was the old witch Malgotha herself.

Cheesewire couldn't believe it when he saw her. A small black creature with the crumpled face and body of an old mole, the nose and paws of a shrew, and a look in her eye that was all rat. Her very long mud-coloured tail could have belonged to anything.

"Feast your eyes, little squitter!" she hissed. "Am I not a vision of the purest splendour?"

The mouse frowned.

"No," he said—and the old witch laughed.

"No? Well now, boy, you do surprise me!" Then her face and tone of voice changed completely. She became angry and urgent and crawled right up close to the white mouse. Even though she was smaller than him, he couldn't help stepping back a pace.

"No," she said, touching his face with flecks of spittle. "No, boy, I'm not a splendid thing. I'm old and withered and I look like shit. But for all that, I'm still Malgotha. I can do things no-one else can do, and I know everything. Everything, boy—do you understand?"

Cheesewire didn't, but he thought it best to nod his head.

"I know everything and everyone, boy. Your name and everything about you, though you've never seen my face. And I know why you're here."

"Well, that saves me explaining it, then," said the mouse brightly.

"Your insolence no longer amuses me, sprat!" snarled Malgotha. She came and stood very close to him. He could smell her breath on his face as she talked, and he half-turned his head to avoid it.

"So, my little bantam," she growled, "if you've no more jibes, we'll get down to business. You and your friends need the craft of Malgotha to save your darling forest, don't you? Well then, listen to me. Two things: first, let me tell you I've no great love for the forest and those who live in it, just as they have no love for me—so my help will be limited. And secondly, you will at least have some help. I'll destroy the great crocodile for you— at a price."

"Crocodile?" said Cheesewire. "You mean the big lizard?"

"He's no lizard, puppy. They call him the Mugger crocodile where he comes from."

"Where's that?"

"It's not for you to know!" snapped the witch. "The horror crocodile is here, that's the important thing. And he'll eat you out of house and home unless I stop him. Well, stop him I shall—but the forest will have to pay for my services." She paused. Cheesewire scratched his hip and said nothing. "Your friends think I'm some kind of conjuror, a purveyor of spells—but if they think I can make the Mugger disappear in a cloud of smoke, they're very wrong. I can show you how to kill the crocodile, boy—but the rest you'll have to do yourself, on your own."

"What, me?" gasped the mouse. "What can I do? You must be mad—"

"Hold your tongue, brat!" she growled, and punched him on the nose with her wrinkled fist, making his eyes water. He put his paws over his face and looked at her through his fingers.

"Listen again," she said, tugging his fur to pull him closer. "It's all down to you now. You alone can lure the

Mugger to his death—and you alone can pay my price."

Cheesewire sniffed and smelt blood in his nose. He wiped some of it away with his finger.

"What can you want from me?" he asked. "I've got nothing to give you."

Malgotha smiled only with her lips.

"You're wrong, boy. You've got everything I want. Your life, little shit! Your own skin. In return for the Mugger's head, I want your life—and your death."

The mouse stood quite still and stared at her, heard everything she said but couldn't believe it. He didn't say a word.

"Ah, so the chattermouse is lost for words at last!" The witch had a grin on her face, showing a smattering of soft brown teeth. "You thought it was all a joke, didn't you, blondie? A day out, a chance to see the old black witch for yourself. Now you know, clever boy—the Mugger is no laughing matter. And nor is Malgotha."

The mouse bowed his head.

"What do you want me to do?" he asked.

"First of all you have to make a choice, cub. You can walk out of here, forget about the crocodile, and stay alive as long as you can (after all, why put your foot in the snare? You owe the forest as little as I do) or you can find the great beast and do as I tell you. But if you find him and kill him, you must return here that same day and pay your debt—or I'll come looking for you myself. And if I do, your death will be as slow as the river."

Cheesewire scratched his nose as he waited for her to continue.

"Now listen for the last time, whelp. If you want the Mugger to die, you must lead him down to the Rooted Caverns near the mouth of the Great River . . ."

And the big young mouse stood with his head bowed, listening, nodding, and feeling rather sorry for himself, the blood seeping from his nose to stain the fur on his paws below, while the black hybrid witch went on talking till the stone vault was dark again and it was time for him to leave.

When the old hag ordered him out of her lair, night had already fallen—and Cheesewire lost no time in putting a fair distance between himself and the grey hills. He went on running along the edge of the river until his lungs began to hurt him. Then he stopped and rested behind a tussock of grass.

His nose had stopped bleeding but there was a crust of blood around his nostrils and a pale bruise under one eye. He felt shaken and subdued—and he still had a choice to make. To forget the whole thing and stay alive, or go back and face the crocodile. It wasn't much of a choice, and he made his mind up very quickly. Before long he was up and trotting briskly back to the forest.

First he had to pass through the land of the gorse bushes, where the last brown rats were living. In the darkness his white fur made him an easy target, and he decided there was no point trying to sneak through unseen. So he ran, like a mad hare, sprinting and weaving, running harder every time he saw a shadow move. More than once he thought he heard a curse or a whisper, the sound of fast footsteps—but in the end he was free of the barren place. Before dawn he was back in the land of the Lonely Trees.

From here it was still a long walk to the edge of the forest, and it was daytime before he arrived there. As he hurried along the riverbank, he did a lot of looking around. Keeping an eye open for the big reptile, but also looking hard at the forest itself. The shapes and colours, the assortment of trees. He found himself smiling at the good things: the dark elms with their buttresses and thick ribs of bark; the thick wet river-mud like brown cottage cheese; a small hawk moth fluttering down from the trees like a pair of welded sycamore seeds. Normally the white mouse wouldn't have given all this a second thought, but just now he couldn't help it. It was strange to think he'd never see any of it again.

And yet it didn't bother him too much. He didn't want to die, but he'd had his fun and was ready to pay for it. It was an unusual way of thinking but it was the way he looked at things so that was that. As for death itself, well, he knew one thing: it wouldn't be boring.

He ran on along the riverbank, but the crocodile was nowhere to be seen—so he moved away to try his luck in the forest itself. The lizard wasn't there either, but it had left its mark. The mouse passed more than one half-eaten body or pile of bones. In fact it seemed to him that the whole floor of the forest was littered with signs of death and decay. Broken branches, dead leaves, rotting ferns, a vast brown carpet of pine needles. And the parasites, feeding on death: the woodlice and beetles, the ivy, moss, and fungus. A whole world built on dead things. Cheesewire had never thought of it like that before.

"Don't be so daft, Cheese," he scolded himself. "Keep your mind on what you're doing."

That was easier said than done, but it didn't matter, because before long he saw something that drove all other thoughts out of his head.

He inched his nose round the side of a dappled plane tree—and there it was, lying on its belly in a grassy clearing between the trees, basking in the heat with its eyes shut and its mouth wide open, showing a rash of huge teeth. The killer crocodile, the Mugger himself. Sun-bathing.

Cheesewire stood quite still for a while, giving himself time to calm down and remember what to do next. Then he took two huge deep breaths and marched out into the clearing, right in front of the crocodile.

The reptile was half-asleep and didn't notice him, so he coughed to attract its attention. Nothing happened. The mouse moved a little closer.

"Hey you!" he cried. "Wake up, Muggins. I want a word with you!"

This time the massive jaws moved. The crocodile closed them, bringing them together very slowly. The huge long eyes opened and stared at the mouse. From the back of its throat came a harsh warning hiss.

Cheesewire wasn't surprised when he saw from the look in its eye that the giant reptile had recognised him. When it first moved into the forest, the mouse had started to play with it, running around its vast great body, dodging its teeth and claws until he grew tired of the game and went off to try something else. From the way it looked at him he guessed that the monster remembered all this and was quite ready to teach him a lesson.

But then it seemed to lose interest in him, shutting its eyes and going back to sleep, its teeth showing through the closed jaws in a savage grin. The mouse realised he'd have to try a little harder.

"Now look here, Muggins," he called out, "we can't go on like this. There's rules in this forest, you know—and one of them says no-one can go to sleep when the great Cheesewire is talking. So wake up and pay attention or I'll have to come and sort you out."

The monster ignored him.

"Right then," he said grimly. "You asked for it." And in one burst of movement he dashed across the grass, jumped, landed, ran up along the crocodile's snout, and stood on the top of its head.

"Anybody in there?" he shouted, knocking on its skull with his fist.

The crocodile didn't like that. It gave a loud heavy-throated grunt, jerked its body upwards and twisted to one side, throwing the mouse through the air. As Cheesewire hit the ground, the Mugger was already on its feet looking for him—but he rolled away through the grass, recovered his balance, and rushed off to the foot of the nearest tree.

His pulse was very loud in his ears as he turned and saw the crocodile scratching at the grass near its feet. Its mouth was half-open and he didn't like the expression on its face.

"I'm over here, Muggerbugger!"

The huge thing turned its head and saw him. It gave another deep grunt and came lumbering across the clearing towards him. When Cheesewire ran away, it followed him.

And followed him. Between the trees, across a meadow, back into the forest, across a row of thin black ditches, always with the white mouse not too far ahead but just out of reach—and the enormous crocodile clumping along behind him, high on its legs, its fat body swaggering from side to side as it waddled after him.

And so Cheesewire led the killer beast towards the mouth of the river. Just as it seemed on the point of giving up this long tantalising chase, he jumped into the fast-moving flood and set off downstream. As he hoped, this put new heart into the reptile, for it knew it could outpace the mouse in any race through water.

It slid on its belly down the muddy bank, kicking with its feet to push itself into the water. Then, with its legs pressed against the sides of its body, it set off in pursuit, relying on its thick tail and webbed hind feet to drive it along the river. Cheesewire glanced back over his shoulder and saw the reptile gaining on him very quickly, only its eyes and nostrils showing above the surface. He smiled. He was beginning to enjoy himself again. It was his first taste of amusement since the two days he'd spent living in a beehive, and he began to savour the excitement of the chase.

The crocodile was almost within striking distance by the time the mouse reached a point where the river raced sharply downhill, speeding over a low pile of rocks. The two animals went hurtling down through the noise and the spray and the rounded boulders, down to where the river levelled out—then further on, to the rim of another water-fall.

This was much steeper than the first, a long cascading drop covered with a permanent steam of cold spray. Cheesewire made sure he led the crocodile along the left-hand side. Down he went, the reptile following close on his tail, reaching for him with its jaws. It had no fear of the fast water.

Near the foot of the waterfall, the left bank of the river was overhung by the roots of two huge oak trees. Great twisting roots, old as the forest itself. Hundreds of them in a vast fibrous meshwork, forming a maze of wooden chambers that the creatures of the forest called the Rooted Caverns. Cheesewire had been there twice before. He found it a thrilling, terrifying place.

Everything seemed to happen at once. There was a roaring in his ears as he was dragged underwater, and the force of the current crashed his head and body against one hard root after another. Then, before he knew what was happening, the torrent had swept him down through the Caverns to the quiet stretches near the sea, driving him through a wide wooden tunnel filled to the ceiling with rabid riverwater.

The tunnel was wide—but only for the mouse. It was just a little too thin for the crocodile—but by the time he realised that, it was too late. He couldn't fight the pace of the water and it thrust him head-first into the tunnel like a stopper into a bottle, leaving only the gaps above and below his flat body for the water to rush through. He gave a short grunt of pain as his flanks were jammed against the sides of the passage. He tried to roar but the water filled his mouth. He kicked and scrabbled with his feet, strained with his huge armoured muscles—but the pressure of the water held him firmly in place. Before very long his eyes began to bulge till they seemed on the point of bursting. Then his lungs began to receive their first draughts of water. By the time Cheesewire had scampered back up to see how things had turned out, the great Mugger was well and truly dead. His tail and short fat hind legs were sticking out of the rushing water, and they looked anything but dangerous.

The wild water had washed away the crust of blood from Cheesewire's nose but the wound had been re-opened during his fall down the rapids. He let it bleed. There were more important things to think about.

First of all he ran off to find Reek the squirrel and told him the news. Then, while Reek and his uncle and a flock of other animals hared off to the waterfall, the mouse went away along the riverbank towards Malgotha's den. Soon his forelegs and chest had changed colour as his nose dripped freely all over them.

When he reached the first of the Lonely Trees, he heard a noise behind him and turned round. The black witch was there, crouched under a root. There was a small smile on her face.

"So, little maggot, the great Mugger didn't drink your brains after all. Your luck's held out very well."

Cheesewire looked at the ground.

"Well, it's run out now," he sulked. The witch didn't answer. "I wasn't trying to run away," he added. "I was coming to see you."

"Yes, blondie, I know that. I told you: I know everything."

"Then why are you here?" he demanded. "You couldn't wait, I suppose. Perhaps you could smell the blood on my face."

Malgotha came up to him.

"Blood, Master Cheese?" she said quietly. "What blood?"

He frowned at her. There was another smile on her long face, a friendly smile. He looked down at his chest. There was no blood on it. His legs were white again too, and all the tiredness had left them. He looked up.

"No, little droppings," said Malgotha, "I don't want your life. If I did, I'd have taken it when you came to see me. But the task of destroying the Mugger had to be yours. You were the only one in the forest who could do it."

"I don't see why," said the mouse sullenly. "And I can't

understand why you didn't tell me that before instead of playing stupid games with me."

"You had to be tested, Master Cheese."

"Why?"

"That's not for you to know!" snapped the witch. "And even if you knew, it wouldn't change anything. You've done what you were set to do and you're still alive. Beyond that, there's nothing that concerns you."

Cheesewire puffed out his cheeks and shook his head. He was still trying to take it all in.

"Now I'm going home," said the hag. "But I'll be back. There are things to be finished. Meet me where the Mugger's body lies, ten days from now."

"What for?"

"Do as you're told, grub!—before I change my mind and suck your eyes out. Now go back to the forest and spread the word: in ten days I'll be back, at noon, by the wide waterfall. Let those who have enough pluck be there with me—and tell them to leave the reptile's stomach alone."

And with that strange instruction she hobbled off along the riverbank and disappeared behind the first knock-kneed willow.

The witch was true to her word. Within the ten days she was standing near the edge of the second waterfall, watching from the far bank as the river crashed down on the trapped remains of the monster crocodile. Only the great white bones were left now, gleaming like snares in the sun, a playpen for ducklings. The rats and voles and small pike, and especially the birds, had stripped away all the skin and meat. Only the entrails had been left untouched.

Malgotha turned to the crowd of animals behind her. Most of them avoided her eyes.

"Fetch me the Mugger's stomach, one of you. Take out the bones you find there and bring them up to the first flat stretch of the river."

The largest of the otters slid into the river and skimmed across to the other side. The black witch turned and shuffled off up the steep bank. The other animals followed her, keeping their distance.

After a while, the otter came trotting along the grass to join the rest of the crowd, carrying a bundle of bones in its mouth. It laid them gently at Malgotha's feet then stepped back to stand with the others and shake itself dry.

The old witch was left to stand on her own, a few paces away, closer to the water's edge. For a time she did nothing except stare at the bones, and while she did so nobody moved or dared to speak. Reek frowned enquiringly at his uncle, his uncle frowned at Cheesewire, and the white mouse shrugged.

Then the witch bent down and rummaged through the litter of bones with her long nose, picking at them with her paws. She pushed the very longest bone to one side, then gathered up the others in her mouth, carried them to the river, and dropped them in.

Nothing happened. No-one expected anything to happen. The witch leaned out over the edge of the bank and spat on the water below. Then she mumbled a string of strange words and pointed at the water with a long naked finger, her tail slushing in the mud behind her.

Still nothing happened, and the bunch of animals grew restless, chattering and muttering and whispering as they nudged each other and frowned at Malgotha's back.

And then, quite suddenly, they fell silent again. They watched as the river water started to boil and tumble, hissing and splashing against the bank. From under the waves came a deep heavy rumbling sound, the ground began to shudder—and out of the river itself, in a daub of colour, bounded a small army of different animals, soaked to the skin and laughing like jackdaws.

All the old victims of the Mugger were there, once dead and now very much alive. Mice and rats and rabbits and pigeons, a bullfinch, a coot, a ferret, and three moorhens. And one small, rather stout, rather short-sighted vole.

"Well, gouge me!" laughed the three-legged badger. "It's old Vim!"

And so it was—but before anyone had a chance to greet him, there was a loud bellow—and another, larger, female vole came striding through the grass.

"There you are at last, you idle old scrounger!" she thundered, thumping Vim's shoulder with her nose. "And where do you think you've been all this time?"

"I think I've been dead, my dear," answered Vim, reasonably enough.

"Oh, and I suppose you think that's a good reason for doing nothing, don't you? Any excuse to leave me on my own—me with an army of little ones to bring up! Just you wait till I get you home!"

And without another word she marched the old vole away along the bank. She went on scolding him all the way back to their burrow, but she walked with her nose in his fur and a big grin on her mouth. Vim's famous good luck had come back to him, and the rest of the crowd laughed and cheered as they watched him leave.

Then the riverbank was filled with crying and laughter and animals jumping around welcoming everyone home—

until the voice of the old hag cut across the uproar and there was silence.

"Be still, all of you!" she hissed. "I have other work to do."

Again she walked to the river's edge, this time with the last, largest bone in her teeth. She let it fall. Once again the waters swelled and grumbled, there was another dark trembling noise—and out of the depths, in a burst of satin brown and red, came the great lord Arcan, as bright and glossy as a chestnut.

His son was the first to greet him, then the heron, Bell-hop the rabbit, and the frog, then all the other beasts, nuzzling his body with their snouts and climbing on his back.

"Do you think I should tell him it wasn't a badger that killed him?" said the badger with three legs. Reek smilingly shook his head.

"I think he probably knows that already," he said.

"Hm," said the badger. "Yes, perhaps you're right." And Reek, his uncle, and Rusalka laughed and patted the badger's shoulder.

The Stag was happy to share the crowd's high spirits for a while, but soon he moved away and walked over to the black witch. As the other animals watched in silence, he bowed his head in front of her.

"So, old mother," he said, "the ancient prophecies have come to pass."

"Yes," she nodded. "As we both knew they would be."

They smiled, rather solemnly, at each other.

"And you too, little white one, great deliverer of the forest—you will never be forgotten."

Cheesewire felt very honoured. He thought he ought to

say something in return, but all he could do was smile and look happy and roll his eyes.

"And your courage shall not go unrewarded," continued the High Stag. "As long as you live, any bush you choose will wear an apron of the very best strawberries, for you and all your companions."

The mouse twitched his long ears and put a wide greedy grin on his face. He bowed with his head.

"That sounds a fair price to me!" he said.

Things were back to normal after that. The animals went on with their lives and Malgotha became their friend. Most of her time was spent with the white mouse, either in her hillside den or in the forest, where they could stroll and eat strawberries and swim in the river.

She even managed to cure his squint.